D1236653

THE LEGEND OF NANCE DUDE

THE LEGEND OF NANCE DUDE

by Maurice Stanley

JOHN F. BLAIR, PUBLISHER
WINSTON-SALEM, NORTH CAROLINA

This book is printed on acid-free paper.

Library of Congress Cataloging-in-Publication Data

Stanley, Maurice, 1945–
The legend of Nance Dude / by Maurice Stanley.
p.   cm.
ISBN 0-89587-081-9 (cloth : acid-free paper)
1. Kerley, Nancy Ann, 1848–1952—Fiction.
2. North Carolina—History—1865– —Fiction.   I. Title.
PS3569.T3333L44   1991
813'.54—dc20
90-23886

To
Louise Stanley
my mother

I have you fast in my fortress,
And will not let you depart,
But put you down into the dungeon
In the round-tower of my heart.

And there will I keep you forever,
Yes, forever and a day,
Till the wall shall crumble to ruin,
And moulder in dust away.

Henry Wadsworth Longfellow
"The Children's Hour"

Acknowledgments

The Legend of Nance Dude is based on a true story that happened in Waynesville, North Carolina, in 1913. It was reported at that time in the old *Waynesville Courier* and again in 1923 in the book *The Serpent Slips into a Modern Eden* by James A. Turpin. My thanks go to Clifton B. Metcalf, editor of the *Waynesville Mountaineer*, for making the relevant issues of the *Courier* available to me, and to John Parris, senior editor of the *Asheville Citizen*, for telling me about the Turpin book.

For information about Nance Dude's imprisonment I am indebted to James Sorrell, archivist for the North Carolina Department of Cultural Resources; Sam Garrison, historian of Raleigh's Central Prison; and especially William Rolen, Swain County magistrate.

I am much obliged to Clara Belle Palmer, Jack Best, Luther Best (now deceased), Hobart Franklin, Naomi Franklin (deceased), Wilma Conner Gray and all the other mountain people who were kind enough to share their memories of the story with me.

Thanks to my parents, Claude and Louise Stanley, who traipsed with me around Waynesville and Bryson City from Jonathan's Creek to Conley's Creek, through courthouses and cemeteries and even up the side of

Utah Mountain to the little cave where Roberta Ann Putnam was murdered, for helping me put together Nance's sad, dark story.

Thanks to Steve Kirk, my editor at John F. Blair, for his thorough, intelligent and sensitive work on *The Legend of Nance Dude*, and for his encouragement.

Above all, thanks to my wife, Glana, for her care, for never forsaking me, and for typing and proofreading several drafts of this and other books of mine. Ours.

THE LEGEND OF NANCE DUDE

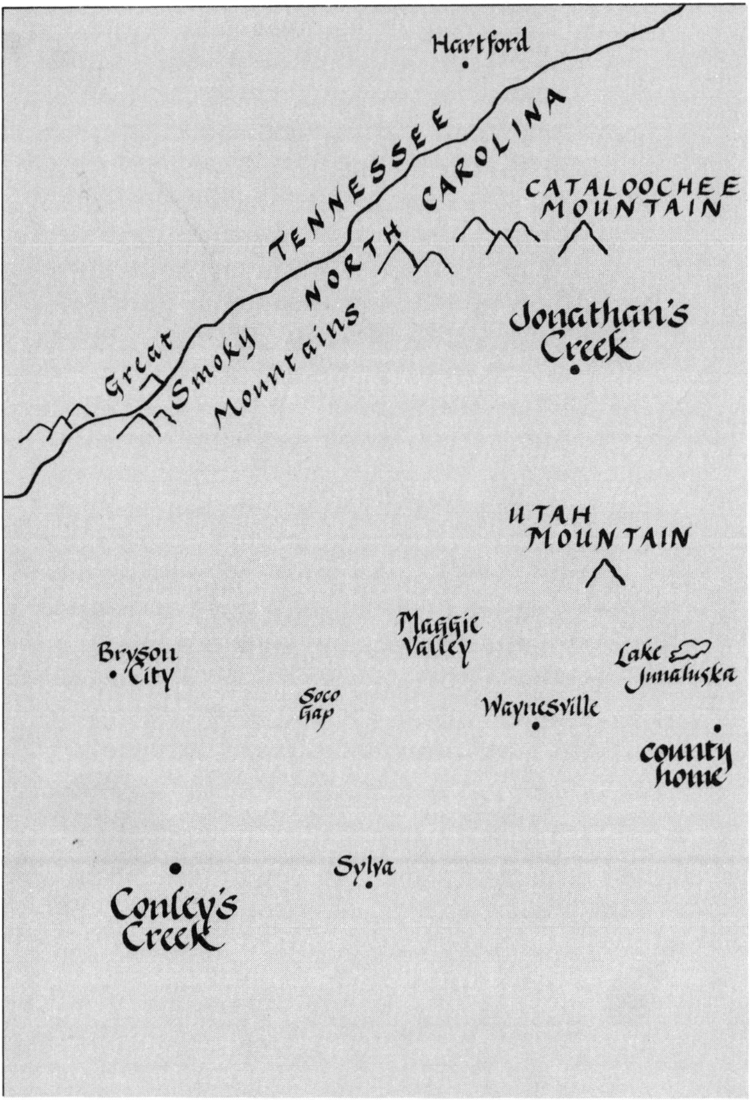
Hartford
TENNESSEE
NORTH CAROLINA
Great Smoky Mountains
CATALOOCHEE MOUNTAIN
Jonathan's Creek
UTAH MOUNTAIN
Maggie Valley
Bryson City
Lake Junaluska
Soco Gap
Waynesville
county home
Sylva
Conley's Creek

Prologue

About forty people showed up Tuesday morning, April
8, 1913, at the Jonathan's Creek Baptist Church at the
foot of Utah Mountain to look for the little girl. The
photographer was there from Waynesville with his big
tripod camera, and he set the searchers down at the edge
of the woods and took their picture.

Most of the residents of Jonathan's Creek were there. There was old Jase Ledford, who had once loved Nance Dude with all his heart; and his wife, Lucille; and his pretty daughter, Joellen, the new schoolteacher; and the man Joellen loved, Birch Phillips; and Birch's father, Zeb, who had brought along some moonshine for the menfolk. And some kids, among them Aaron Hatley, fifteen; and his sweetheart, Lois Ransom; and his worst enemy, Frank Janes; and Frank's dog, Peedro. And lots more people besides, from all over Haywood County, all thrilled at the gravity of the project, all hoping and dreading to find little Roberta Ann Putnam.

After the photo session, while the searchers were gathered in one spot, Deputy Jack Carver addressed them: "We'll need to do this systematically, neighbors. I want about half of you to take the bottom half of this side of the mountain. You need to stick close to the road. Nance is a old woman, so I figure she didn't put the child too far off the path. The rest of you," he said, gesturing toward the right half of the party, "will go up and search the top. The child was—is—about two and a half. She's blond and right pale, as I understand. If she's been, well, killed, she'll be covered up by leaves, I'd say, or maybe completely buried. Don't get lost! We don't want to wind up hunting for you, too.

"And there's snakes up in there, just waking up, and maybe bears. So go in two at a time, and watch where you put your feet."

He had plainly thought this out in advance, and the

people all felt proud of him. He was a good man, a sensible man.

So the searchers strode off up the road. Several of the men had rifles and others had shotguns. One old man had a musket he'd carried in the Civil War.

Aaron Hatley ran to catch up with Lois Ransom and walk beside her. She gave him a shy smile. She knew very well how he felt about her.

"Sure hope we find her alive," Aaron said.

"Daddy says we won't. He figures that old Nance killed her and buried her. That's what he says."

The morning sunlight shining through the limbs and leaves of the trees that lined the little wagon road up the side of the mountain caused Aaron to squint and grin. "She might be alive," he said. "Ain't no call to give up hope yet."

"She's been gone for over a month," Lois said. "I don't see how she could still be alive. What's she been eating? And it's been cold. Or maybe snakes have eaten her, or maybe a bear." She shivered.

Up came Frank Janes and Peedro to join them, to Aaron's dismay. "Reckon we'll find that poor youngun?" Frank asked cheerfully. Peedro licked at Lois's hand. Aaron hated Frank and his stupid mixed-breed dog.

"Reckon old Nance done it? *I* believe she did," Frank jabbered. "I believe she's a witch, that's what I believe! It'd take a old witch to kill her own grandbaby. That's what my Aunt Sues figures. I figure she's right. You know, Nance *looks* like a witch to me."

"There's no such thing as witches," Lois said. Aaron felt a swell of love for her, for her prettiness and her good sense.

"There is, too! And Nance Dude is one, I'm sure of that. Aunt Sues says she used to see Nance peeling bark off of walnut trees, and that's a sure sign. What they do is, they take little innocent babies and cut them up and offer them up to the devil! I reckon that's what Nance Dude has done, and so I figure we won't find nothing of that child, except maybe pieces."

"That's dumb as hell," Aaron said, watching Lois's face. She grinned.

"Who you calling dumb?" Frank asked, his face getting red. "I'll kick your ass for you, short-life." All three stopped. No adults were around. Frank was two years older and a foot taller than Aaron, but Aaron was plucky. The two boys squared off.

"We got to find Roberta Putnam," Lois said sternly, walking between them. "Now come on. Let's go up that bank yonder. She could be in there."

The boys followed Lois, watching each other. Lois scrambled up the bank, pushing through tall weeds and bushes. Over the crest of the bank they came upon a patch of leaves. Lois dug into it with her hands.

"Hey!" Aaron said. "You'll get snakebit for sure! Use a stick or something." Frank broke a limb off a young hickory tree and Lois and Aaron stepped back as he dug into the leaves. There were only wet leaves packed beneath the dry ones. The three looked at one another in relief and disappointment.

Up the road Jase Ledford, who was sixty-three, poked at the bushes beside the road with his cane. His wife, Lucille, was chattering, "I shouldn't of worn this dress. I shouldn't of come at all. Those Putnams are really quite beneath us, as I've always told you, Jase. Haven't I always told you that? You should *never* have let that awful old woman live on our land! I know this will kill my mother. She's sick and old and I know it will just finish her off. Everybody knows about it, everybody's talking about it. Do you realize people are even saying she's a *witch*?"

"Your mama?"

"No! Oh, you are just . . . unregenerate! The Bible says, 'The unregenerate lusted after wickedness, and were lost.'"

Up ahead of the others Deputy Jack Carver and his friend Dave Leatherwood probed the bushes and weeds and peered into the shadows among the dense foliage. Dave was a silent man whom Jack always deputized when he needed real help. Jack trusted him.

"What could have made that old woman do such a thing?" Jack asked. "If she did it, I mean?"

Dave shook his head and pushed back some bushes with the barrel of his .30-30. Nothing there.

"I mean, Nance and the Putnams aren't hardly the cream of society, but that don't explain anything."

Dave didn't respond. He never did. But he was there, and he listened.

Jack considered the evidence. Nance had been seen with her granddaughter going up the mountain the morning of the day the girl turned up missing, and she was seen later that same day coming back down. Alone. That was about all anybody really knew. That didn't prove she killed the little girl.

But the lies, the lies! For one, Nance had told her daughter, Lizzy, the child's mother, that she took the girl to the county home. But the child wasn't at the county home. And then there was the story about the man in black.

So Nance was a liar, but that didn't make her a murderer. And yet Jack was sure the child was dead, and had been dead for a month.

He wiped his forehead with the sleeve of his coat. It was a spring day that had started out cold and now was warming up.

"I've been a deputy in this county for eleven years," he said to Dave as he scratched at a suspicious-looking pile of leaves. "I've never seen a case like this. What in God's name would make a sixty-five-year-old woman do something like this?"

His stick prodded something leathery and softly resistant under the leaves and he froze. "Hey! Jesus!" he said. A pungent odor of decayed flesh slapped at his nostrils and his eyes focused on a small, round ball of hair. He swallowed and rubbed his nose and turned around in embarrassment toward Dave, who was looking at him.

"Possum," he said. "Dead possum."

Nance Dude sat in the county jail on the second floor of the old courthouse in Waynesville. On the bunk across the cell her very pregnant daughter, Lizzy, lay asleep. In the adjoining cell Will Putnam sat whittling. Deputy Jack had decided it was okay for Will to have a pocketknife. Jack was a compassionate man.

Will was whittling a dog—a hound dog with long ears. He liked dogs. He despised chickens, hogs, goats, horses and cattle, all the farm animals that belonged to rich Jase Ledford, animals he had to feed and take care of. He did not despise Mr. Ledford, of course. Mr. Ledford was a fine man, a gentleman who had let the Putnams live on his land since before Will was born.

Will glanced over at Nance, who was wedging a big pinch of snuff between her bottom gum and lip. Her eyes met his and he looked away.

He hated her. He feared her.

Nance looked out the window at the April sky and sucked at her snuff and spat into the spit-can Jack had given her. He had brought her the snuff, too. She could hear people talking outside, down on the street. She got up and went to the window and looked through the bars at the little crowd below.

"Look!" some woman cried out. "There she is!"

"Sorry old bitch!" a man shouted.

"She needs hanging!" the woman demanded.

"Murderer!" another man hollered, and a clod of dirt flew through the bars past Nance's head and exploded on the wall beside her. She went back to her bunk and sat down.

"Mama?" Lizzy said, and sat up, holding her huge belly. "What was that?"

"Somebody throwed a clod of dirt in," Nance said.

"Why would they want to do something like that?" Lizzy asked.

Nance did not reply. She was hungry and she hoped it wouldn't be long till Mrs. Sizemore, the cook at the Waynesville Cafe, brought their supper. Mrs. Sizemore was a fine cook and the meals she brought were good.

Nance folded her arms over her skinny breasts and tried to think how she would answer all the questions. The lies were hard to keep straight but if she told the truth people wouldn't understand. They would hang her for sure.

It was the worst bind she had ever been in. But she intended to survive.

Chapter One

In 1858 Nance was ten years old. She was a happy child who loved her little brother, Elmer. One June day she was playing house with him in the dirt behind the Conard cabin, beside the hog lot. It had rained that afternoon and the ground was moist.

"You hold the baby while I wash his britches," Nance said, handing Elmer a rotting turnip with sticks stuck in it for arms and legs.

"What's his name?" Elmer asked.

"Turnip-top," Nance said, and they both giggled.

Twenty feet away, in the darkness of the woods, something moved. Nance heard it and looked up but at first she saw nothing. Then whatever it was made a sniffing, woofing noise, and a part of the forest took sudden shape. It was big, with black eyes and nose and yellow teeth that Nance would never forget. It stood on its massive hind legs and looked at the two children for a moment, then lumbered toward them.

Nance screamed and jumped up and scrambled away toward the back door of the cabin. Elmer twisted around and looked at the beast and laughed and put out his chubby hand toward it. It reared up and growled.

John and Kathleen came running around the side of the house from the front porch. Nance fell across the back steps and looked over her shoulder. She watched, and so did John and Kathleen, as the beast put its heavy paw on Elmer's small body and held him down and then bit into his leg and tore at it.

Elmer screamed wildly, pitifully. John and Kathleen watched for an awful, frozen moment and then Kathleen ran directly at the bear, hollering helplessly, "*No, no, no! Oh, no!*"

The bear put its huge mouth over Elmer's head, picked him up, turned and, on all fours, ran into the woods.

John ran past Nance into the cabin and grabbed his muzzleloading shotgun and tried to load it, his hands shaking. He cursed as he worked over it and finally he ran out and into the woods after the bear.

Kathleen grabbed Nance up off the back steps, where she was still crouched. "What was you a-doing? You wasn't watching him! He's killed now! Tore up! Our little boy, our onliest boy! Goddamn you, you should of grabbed him and *run*! You didn't do nothing! You just run off and left him! Oh, God, oh!" She shoved Nance away and collapsed in tears. Nance wept miserably.

Then they heard the shotgun blast. They watched for several minutes before John emerged from the woods carrying Elmer. The boy was utterly limp, his arms and legs dangling comically. His head and leg dripped blood.

"Is he . . . ?"

"He's alive," John said. "The bear dropped him when I shot at it. I don't know if I hit it or not." He looked at the boy. "His leg is tore up bad, and his face. And his eye."

Kathleen looked and went pale. Nance was beside her trembling and sobbing. Elmer's left eye was gouged out and his face was ripped and there was an ugly hole in his forehead at the hairline that was bleeding badly.

"Get away!" Kathleen hissed at Nance. "You've done enough, don't you reckon? Oh, dear Jesus, he's ruint!" The thought passed through her mind that she should have been watching the children herself. But it was easier to blame Nance. Nance went back and sat down on the steps, crying.

"His leg is eat plumb off," Kathleen said to John. "You got to take him to Doc Crawford in Waynesville."

John got the plow horse and put a bridle on it while Kathleen wrapped some clean gingham around Elmer's head and leg. He came to and started wailing with pain.

His right kneecap and shinbone were showing. John lifted him onto the horse and rode off down the Indian trail toward Waynesville.

Nance sat on the back steps and cried until she got hiccups and then went into the house to the cot where she and Elmer slept. She cried and cried until she went to sleep.

Young Doc Crawford washed Elmer's leg in alcohol to kill infection and bandaged it neatly. Then he swabbed out the eye and the head wound and bandaged them, too.

"The eye's ruined, I'm afraid," he told John. "I think the leg will heal, but it'll take a long time. I expect he'll have a limp. But he'll live. He's lucky." He suspected there was brain damage but he said nothing to John about it. "It must have picked him up by the head," he said. "He's lucky to be alive."

The next day John and some other men from Jonathan's Creek went up through the woods on the east side of Cataloochee Mountain hunting the bear. They were rich old William Ledford and one of his slaves, Billy, who could shoot; and Zeb Phillips, who ran the Jonathan's Creek general store; and Joe Putnam, who squatted on the Ledford farm; and Dude Hannah and Howard Kerley, just boys. But they had no luck. The woods were deep and dark and they could hardly see to walk.

Elmer's leg was no good after that, nor his eye. And as time went by it became plain that he would never be very smart. He grinned too much and his face was terribly scarred and monstrous-looking and he was slow to understand. And Nance blamed herself for all of it. She had been a pleasant girl but now she grew surly and backward. She knew she should have *done* something, as her mother said, but she had done nothing and now Elmer was ruined. When she looked at him she wished the bear had got her instead.

Elmer's scars were out where you could see them. Nance's were deeper, in her heart.

Chapter Two

Dust was rising and there was noise in the distance.
Nance, Elmer, Jase Ledford and Jane Putnam were
crouched in the tall weeds and dead cornstalks in a field
where they had been playing hide-and-seek. They listened and watched the road.

"What do you reckon it can be?" Jane asked. She was a

year or two older than Nance and had a husband, Joe, somewhere up north in the Confederate army. She was simpleminded and good-natured and still enjoyed childish games.

"A bunch of horses," Nance said. She broke off a bit of cornstalk and put it in the corner of her mouth. The cornfield was grown up even though it was plowing time because the war had taken all the men away.

Suddenly Elmer popped up and pointed. "Lookit! Lookit!" he hollered before Nance and Jase pulled him back down. Nance clamped her hand over his mouth. He wiggled and wiggled. He was now eleven but had the mind of a five-year-old.

A line of men in blue uniforms appeared, some on foot and some on horseback. One man was carrying an American flag.

"Yankees," Jase whispered. "They're wearing blue. Rebs wear gray."

"They going to kill us," Elmer said, grinning.

"Naw," Nance said. "They're hunting for Rebs. They ain't after us."

"Ain't we Rebs?" Jane asked.

"Naw. We ain't nothing," Nance said.

They watched the soldiers go by for over half an hour. There were ten men abreast and Jane counted some fifty rows.

"They look plumb wore out," Jane said.

A wagon came along behind the soldiers. It carried three soldiers with rifles and three men in regular clothes who were tied hand and foot. One Yankee soldier was fat, with a black, scraggly beard. One was short, with long hair sticking out from under his cap. The third had stripes on his sleeve and seemed to be asleep sitting up. One of the prisoners had a fiddle between his legs.

"That's Dave Medford!" Jane whispered.

"And Feist Janes, and Toby Mackey," Jase said. "They've been took prisoner."

"Shh," Nance said. All four watched as a soldier on horseback rode back to the wagon.

"This is as good a place as any," the soldier said to the men in the wagon. The driver pulled the wagon off into the brush at the side of the road next to the field where Nance and the others were hiding.

"One last song, Reb," the bearded soldier said, cutting Dave Medford's bonds.

Dave rubbed his wrists and then picked up his fiddle and bow. He played and the other two prisoners sang,

> *Goodbye, sweet Liza,*
> *I'm going to leave you.*
> *You know, and I know,*
> *I'm the fellow with the*
> *Dough, dough, dough, dough.*

Dave kept playing as long as he could. Nance and the others watched silently. Only Nance knew what was about to happen. Old Dave, thin and gray but spry, looked to her like a man trying to soak up the last bit of his life like a biscuit in gravy.

The song trailed off finally and the Yankees took the three men out into the grass and shot them one at a time. They stood bravely, except for Toby Mackey, who was only about sixteen. He wept and cried out, *"Oh, Mama!"* as they shot him. He didn't die immediately but groaned and flopped over and over in the grass until the short Yankee soldier reloaded his musket and shot him again.

At that moment Elmer jumped up and hopped through the cornstalks toward the top of the hill. Just over the hill was the Conard cabin. Two miles away was the Ledford mansion.

The Yankees looked up and saw Elmer's head bobbing among the cornstalks. Nance, Jane and Jase held their breath.

"A spy! Another spy!" the bearded soldier hollered, and he and the short one ran through the field after Elmer. The other Yankee from the wagon, the sergeant, saw a good shot, so he aimed and fired, but missed.

Nance knew she had to do something. She jumped up and ran after the soldiers. Jane and Jase stayed down.

The bearded soldier caught Elmer by the arm and jerked him around. Elmer grinned at him and he could tell the boy wasn't all there. At that point Nance hollered, "He ain't no spy! Leave him alone!"

The short one grabbed her around the waist. "Whoa," he said. "Hey, ain't you a skinny, ugly thing!" He looked at the other soldier and grinned. "Reckon we got time . . . ?"

"Too ugly and hateful," the bearded one said. "I couldn't get worked up over her." He turned to Nance. "This your idiot brother?"

Nance quit struggling and the short one released her. She folded her arms across her little breasts and looked down.

"The war's about over," the short one said. "Didn't anybody tell you damn ignorant hillbillies?"

"I don't know nothing about it," Nance said sullenly. "Why'd you shoot old Dave and them for?"

"They were spies. We caught them watching us. Like you."

"Old Dave wasn't no spy," Nance said. "No more than me."

The short one wiped his brow. "These two are too dumb to tell anybody. There's no Rebs around here. Turn them loose, and to hell with them."

"To hell with you, too," Nance spat. They laughed and went back down the hill and climbed into the wagon. They left the three dead men lying where they had fallen.

After the soldiers left, Nance and Elmer went down to where Jane and Jase were hiding. Jase watched Nance coming, her chestnut hair, her coal-black eyes, her scowl. He loved her for her skinny brown arms and legs, and her surly manner, and her courage. But he realized that she was marrying age—"frying size," as Billy, one of the Ledfords' slaves, put it—and he was only fifteen. And Nance was poor.

"Looks like they're a-heading for your house," Nance said to Jase. His mouth fell open. The only people at home were his mother and Billy and the other slaves. His eyes wide and his heart racing, Jase took off running through the cornstalks, over the hill toward his house.

The soldiers indeed stopped at the Ledford plantation. Jase was still almost a mile away when Colonel Kirk and several soldiers dismounted and looked around the yard.

"Go round up all the horses, and the slaves. Don't kill anybody unless you have to," Kirk said. He was a young man but his face was twisted with the anguish of the war.

He took two soldiers with him to the big front door of the mansion. It was locked. "Kick it open," he said. They did, and Kirk went in behind them. A woman in her early thirties, a pretty, elegant woman, stood in the living room, her back against the fireplace mantel. She had a double-barreled muzzleloader pointed at them. Her eyes were like those of a cornered animal.

"Put that gun down, ma'am, and we'll . . ."

The shotgun went off, both barrels, and one of the soldiers' insides exploded. Kirk pulled out his .36 Navy revolver and shot the woman twice. She fell graciously, with a rustle of her crinoline petticoat, and blood poured demurely out of the holes in her left breast onto the oak floor.

Kirk wanted to vomit. "Gather up all the food you can find and load it in the wagon," he told his aide. "Get the slaves to help. Tomorrow we'll set them free."

As Kirk and his aide walked away from the house Jase ran up to the back door, trying to stay out of sight of the soldiers. He went inside and crept through the kitchen.

"Wait, Master Jase," a thin voice said. He stopped, gasping for breath. The door of the pantry opened. It was Suzy Jane, Billy's wife. "You mustn't go in there, Master Jase," she said. "Miss Emily wouldn't want you to go in there."

Jase saw how afraid she was. He was scared, too. *Dear God, let her be all right*, he prayed as he slowly opened the door to the living room.

"You mustn't look, Master Jase," Suzy Jane said, sobbing.

Jase saw the dead Union soldier first, lying sprawled on his back, his insides blown out, and then he saw his mother.

Elmer hopped along beside Nance to the Conard cabin. "Maw! Maw!" he hollered as they came around the cabin to the backyard, where Kathleen was washing clothes in a wooden washtub. "Bunch of men, Maw! A-riding and a-walking. They had blue coats on, Maw!"

"What's all this about, Nance?" Kathleen asked.

"Bunch of Yankee soldiers, I reckon," Nance said.

"They kilt some men, Maw," Elmer went on. He was

grinning and rubbing his head. "We whipped them and they went away."

"Who'd they kill?" Kathleen asked, stopping her scrubbing.

"Dave Medford, and Feist Janes, and Toby Mackey," Nance said. "Claimed they was spies."

"You talked to them? How many was there?"

"Jane said they was five or six hundred."

"My Lord."

"We kilt one of them, Maw," Elmer said. "Nance cussed one and kilt him, dead as hell!"

"Don't use bad language, Elmer. Dave Medford ain't no spy. Why, he couldn't spy my bloomers. Where they at now?"

"Headed for Ledfords' farm," Nance said.

"Lord, Lord," Kathleen said, bowing her head over the washtub. "What are Yankee soldiers doing up in here? There ain't no war up here. The menfolk are all gone. My Lord."

At the Ledford plantation fifteen of Colonel Kirk's men cleaned out the smokehouse of twenty sides of beef, thirty or so sides of pork and a hundred jars of canned meat and vegetables and loaded them all on the wagon. The kitchen at the mansion was too small to allow cooking for six hundred men so the soldiers dug a cook pit in the front yard and put the slaves to work preparing supper.

Suzy Jane had put Jase upstairs in his room. He

watched the soldiers from the window until nightfall and then he watched the stars. The world seemed greatly changed. It had been a happy place and now it was cold and inhospitable and uncivilized.

He also thought about Nance and how she had stood up to the bluecoats. He derived some comfort from the fact that the world still had Nance in it, her skinny arms and legs and her small breasts and frowning little face and surly disposition. Somehow he felt he understood her better now.

The next day Colonel Kirk assembled the slaves and read them the Emancipation Proclamation and then declared them to be free. They thanked him sincerely and nodded and smiled, secretly wondering what in the world they would do and where they would go. After Kirk and the troops left they dug a grave for Mrs. Ledford under the oak tree beside the house. Suzy Jane stood beside Jase and held him gently but firmly while Billy quoted the appropriate scripture, which he knew by heart, about ashes and dust.

"The war will be over soon," Suzy Jane said to Jase. "Then your daddy'll come home. Until then you'll have to be master here."

Then Billy and two others, moaning and weeping, started shoveling dirt onto the pine coffin. "Whoa!" Billy said, and "Whoa!" and the three fell into a mournful rhythm, each shout wrenching Jase's heart. Suzy Jane's wiry little arm held his shoulders. "Whoa!" Billy said, and "Whoa!" on and on, until the task was done.

As Kirk's company passed through Waynesville they met no resistance because the Confederate troops had been sent to Asheville, twenty-five miles east, to fight Major Walter Martin's Union forces.

The first thing Kirk did was send some men to the county jail, a little wood and brick structure beside the courthouse. There was an old black man who was there for some minor theft, along with the town drunk. Kirk's men released the two prisoners and replaced them with the county sheriff and his deputy. Then they went into the stores and houses and took what they could use, or just wanted, and threw the rest out into the street.

Chapter Three

On the afternoon of June 12, 1865, Zeb Phillips looked
out the window of his general store and saw two men

coming down the road into Jonathan's Creek. One was walking and the other was on horseback.

"Maggie!" Zeb hollered to his wife, who was dusting off some of the dry goods. "Look here! Come and look!"

Maggie was a pudgy, lively little woman. "What is it?" she asked, and followed Zeb outside and shielded her eyes from the sun with her feather duster.

"That's William Ledford on the horse," Zeb said. "I can't make out the other one."

"Dude Hannah!" Maggie hollered. "Hey! Dude!"

The two men picked up speed and Zeb and Maggie ran to meet them, laughing and crying at the same time. Dude waved back at them and embraced them.

"Oh, oh," Maggie said, looking at Dude. "You're thin as a ghost." He was so pitiful that she could say no more. Then she looked up at William Ledford's face, which was tight with pain. His left side was wet with blood and corruption. Zeb reached up to him to help him down but he couldn't move and his eyes weren't focused.

"We come by train through Raleigh," Dude said. "Mr. William, he's bunged up pretty bad in his side. He was at Richmond. It was real bad. I was there, too."

The three of them looked at William Ledford, who swayed in the saddle and tried to say something and then slid down off the horse into Zeb's arms.

"Does he know . . . ?" Maggie asked Dude.

"About what?" Dude asked.

"Emily," Zeb said. "She's dead."

"Emily?" William said, trying to focus. "Emily's dead?"

"The Yankees come through in February," Zeb said, holding William's shoulders. "They killed her."

William cried out, a wild, hopeless cry like that of a man being thrown into hell. Dude helped Zeb hold him as he passed out and then they laid him on the grass beside the road.

Zeb looked at Maggie, who was weeping, and put his hand on Dude's shoulder. "Reckon you know about your folks, Dude?"

Dude nodded and wiped his mouth with the back of his hand. "Hey, Maggie, old girl," he said, grinning. "Don't cry now. The war's over."

Zeb went behind the store to the barn and brought out his horse and hitched it to his wagon and led it back around to where the others were. He and Dude laid William into the wagon and then Dude got in.

William opened his eyes, which were deep wells of pain. "Jason, my boy . . . ?"

"He's okay," Zeb said. "You'll see him in a little while. Just lay back and rest." He tied the reins of William's horse to the back of the wagon and then climbed up into the driver's seat.

"Dude," Maggie said, "you come down here and see us soon, okay?"

"Thanks, Maggie," Dude said as Zeb drove away.

The first house they came to was the Conard cabin. Nance was in the backyard hanging out clothes to dry and she watched them pass. Zeb waved at her but she didn't wave back.

"Same old Nance," Dude said, managing a faint chuckle. "She ain't married yet, I don't guess."

"Not Nance," Zeb said.

A couple of miles later they came to the Putnam shack, on the eastern edge of the Ledford plantation.

"Has Joe Putnam come home yet?" Dude asked Zeb.

"No. Jane and her mother-in-law is all that's there. Have you heard anything about him? Is he still alive?"

"I don't have no idea," Dude said.

Just over the hill from the Putnam shack was the Ledford mansion. As Zeb drove the wagon up to the big front door William stirred and pulled himself up to look around. It was a dismal sight. The slave quarters were falling down and weeds had grown up everywhere. As Zeb and Dude were helping William out of the wagon the door opened and out came Billy and Suzy Jane and, behind them, Jase. Jase couldn't believe this bedraggled man was the father he'd said good-bye to three years earlier. The man who had gone off to war was a young, strong, handsome major, tall and proud astride a beautiful Arabian stallion. This man was filthy and almost dead, his splendid uniform in tatters, his eyes full of fear.

"Jason?" William said, trying to stand alone. Jase ran to his father and buried his face in his chest. William embraced his son and tottered and nearly fell but the boy held him up and walked him to the front door. There William paused and looked out at the fresh grave in the yard under the oak tree. With a pitiful cry he pulled away from Jase and walked three steps toward the grave and fell.

Dude and Billy ran to help Jase lift him up and get him into the house. William murmured and continued straining toward the grave until pain slammed him down into darkness.

When they got to the Hannah place Zeb stopped the wagon and Dude climbed down. "Come see us," Zeb said. Dude grinned and waved and Zeb drove away.

Dude walked slowly up the path to the cabin. There were some green tomatoes and squash growing among the grass and weeds. He stopped and looked back at Zeb's wagon, listening to its diminishing clatter. Then he turned to face the silence of the Hannah family home.

The door creaked as he opened it. Dusk was falling and frogs and katydids were starting to chirp. Dude was hungry and realized that he was imagining the smell of his mother's cooking—chicken frying, cornbread baking. He wanted to see her and he half hoped that what he'd been told was a mistake, that it was about someone else's folks. But he knew better.

He looked around the darkening house. It was nearly empty. There was little furniture, only dust and mold. He felt an ember of childish anger flare up within him, anger at his parents for not being there to welcome him home from the war, the awful war, for not being there when he needed them most.

He went into the bedroom and found the old bed his parents had slept in, now broken down. The cot where he had slept was gone. On the bed was a quilt his mother had made. He pulled it back and a hundred vermin scattered—cockroaches, bedbugs, sow bugs, a mouse.

The windows were broken and grass was growing up through cracks in the floor.

"I regret having to inform you that your mother and father have passed away. Your father's heart failed him while he was in his field hoeing potatoes, and your mother pined away in solitude until she contracted pneumonia and died two months later." That was how the minister of Jonathan's Creek Baptist Church had written it and that was how the sergeant had read it to him in the woods of Virginia. With those words his world had been changed from a good and sensible place to a mean, crazy, hateful one. And after that letter he became utterly careless with his life. He killed a score of Yankees and came through without a physical scratch and this persuaded him that life made no sense. He danced amid minie balls and swords and his father had fallen amid new potatoes—gentle, harmless potatoes and fresh dirt. And his mother had pined away.

He looked in the closet and there was nothing, nothing left. Someone had cleaned them out.

He brushed the mattress off and sat on it. He looked down and beside his foot was a small, dark object. A comb. His mother's comb, made of a seashell. Some teeth were broken out and it was crusted over with mold and grime. Caught among its remaining teeth was a strand of gray hair.

Through the broken bedroom window he saw the sun easing down behind Cataloochee. "Mama?" he asked, and waited, as if she might answer him from beyond the sunset. As darkness fell his weeping made a hollow sound in the empty cabin.

In the following weeks other Jonathan's Creek men came home from the war, tired and defeated but glad to be alive. Joe Putnam came home to Jane and his mother, and John Conard returned to Kathleen and Nance and Elmer. Howard Kerley came home to his parents and his three sisters.

Some never came back. Bret Hatley died at Antietam, Teddy Haynes at Gettysburg, Rich Crawford in a Federal prison in Pennsylvania. They were gone forever except in the memories of fiancées, wives, children, parents.

Those who did return tried to fatten up and get their strength back, and then they set about hoeing and clearing the fields, patching up their houses and barns and fences, chopping firewood for the coming winter and harvesting what little the women and children and old men had been able to plant the previous spring. It was work, work, dawn to dark, but there was a certain joy in it, in the realization that they had survived.

In October Major William Ledford died, leaving young Jase to run the estate. And John Conard was so weakened by the dysentery he had contracted in prison that he was unable to work. Kathleen despaired for his life. The work was left to her and Nance and Elmer.

One snowy Saturday that winter in Zeb Phillips's store, where the veterans gathered and sat in straight-backed chairs around the potbellied wood stove, Howard Kerley was in the middle of a story. Howard was twenty-two, with big red ears and a goofy laugh, but he was good-natured and well-liked.

"And that Yankee lieutenant," Howard was saying, "he said the amnesty oath, about swearing to uphold and support the Union and the Constitution and such as that, you know, so Dude, he takes a chaw . . ."

"That Dude!" Zeb snickered.

". . . and then he gives me a chaw . . ."

"Hyaw, hyaw!" Joe Putnam horselaughed.

". . . and Dude, he says, 'I be ready to take that damn-nasty oath,' Dude says, and we commenced the oath, and I swear, I swear to God . . ."

"Damn-nasty, damn-nasty!" went Joe Putnam and Zeb Phillips, knowing the end of the story was coming up, for they had already heard it three times.

". . . that Dude, he says, 'I swear to hump on the Union and on the Constitution,' he says, 'so help me Andrew Johnson!' And then we both spit right on the floor!" Howard's big ears wiggled as he finished the tale.

The three men exploded into hee-hees and yuk-yuks. It was a gleeful moment, and such moments were hard to come by on Jonathan's Creek in those days. Zeb reached under his counter and brought out a big jug of freshly made corn liquor and passed it around.

"Poor old Dude," Howard said when the merriment subsided. "He keeps a laugh a-going but he hurts inside, I know."

"He's a card," Zeb said. "He can fix anything, build anything. Ain't nobody no smarter. But he won't stay sober. He's never got a cent to his name."

The door opened and the men looked around and there was Nance. She said nothing and didn't smile but brushed the snow from her face and went straight to picking out what she needed. She went first to the flour barrel and dipped out a five-pound sack and then got a five-pound bag of sugar and then a ten-pound sack of chicken feed and finally a ten-pound sack of hog feed. She set each item on the counter in front of Zeb.

"You aim to carry all that, Nance?" Joe asked her, and winked at Howard.

"I reckon," Nance said, barely loud enough to be heard.

"You ought to let young Howard here help you out with that load, Nance," Joe said, grinning at the other men. "He's got a strong back and a weak mind."

"Makings of a good husband," Zeb said.

Howard was embarrassed. "I'll be glad to help you out, Nance," he said, getting up and pulling at the front of his pants.

"Ain't no need," Nance said, and went to the counter and laid out two dollar bills. Zeb counted out her change and handed it to her and she picked up all her purchases and headed for the door. Howard stood looking at her helplessly. Joe gestured for him to go after her, so he followed her out the door and into the snow. The other men chuckled as they left.

"That Nance don't say much," Joe said.

"Nor smile. I never have seen her smile," Zeb said. "She's right handsome, though, in her own way. And she works like a man."

"She don't have much to smile about," Joe said. "The Conards are in right bad shape. John was weakened bad by dysentery in the prison. I doubt if he ever gets over it. He ain't able to do nothing much. Poor Nance does it all, her and her mother."

"Howard would make her a good match, I think," Zeb said.

"He's a good boy. Works hard," Joe said.

"Yep, a good boy," Zeb said, putting the two dollar bills in a drawer under the counter.

Up the road Howard Kerley was carrying the two bags of feed along behind Nance. Snowflakes were falling in his eyes and on Nance's long brown hair.

"Nance?" he said. She didn't answer. "Nance?"

"Yep," she said, not turning to look at him.

"Reckon I could set with you in church tomorrow?"

"I reckon so," she answered, and kept on walking toward home.

———

Howard walked her home after church—a good four miles—and from then on he would sit with her every

Sunday, and at every Wednesday-night prayer meeting, and he would always walk her home. Nance never showed any enthusiasm, but Howard was not discouraged. She never showed her feelings, so nobody could really tell what she felt about anything.

In church Jase Ledford sat alone and saw Nance sitting with Howard. His heart ached for her and he felt bitter but he had no idea of how he might tell her how he felt. Anyway he didn't have time to pursue a romance because of his work rebuilding the plantation. And there was the fact that he was rich and she was poor, and there was what his mother had told him: "The girl is backward, Jase. She's soured. She's got a black cloud setting on her head. She'll never be happy, nor make no man happy."

Still he yearned for her, and it hurt him to see her slipping away into the hands of Howard Kerley. He knew that Howard didn't, couldn't, understand her; somehow Jase felt that Nance was his and would always be his, no matter what. Love had nothing to do with it. It was not a matter of love, but of belonging.

One Sunday in April 1866, after church, Nance and Howard were sitting on the edge of the Conards' porch, their legs hung off.

"Why don't you never smile, Nance?" Howard asked, his ears red.

"Nothing to smile about," Nance said, a twig stuck between her teeth.

"Why, there's *plenty* to smile about, Nance. We're alive,

and dinner's cooking, and we ain't too old to wiggle!"

She just sat and swung her legs back and forth.

"You ever pee off the porch?" he asked.

"Yep," she said.

"No! You can't."

"I reckon I can," she said, and Howard saw a glint in her eye and just a shadow of a smile at the corner of her mouth.

"How?" he asked, grinning.

"I shore can. I can do it standing up."

"Haw, haw, you can't, no more than I can flap my arms and fly."

They sat quietly for a few minutes, listening to Nance's mother stirring up cornmeal in the kitchen, the spoon hitting against the porcelain bowl.

"I never met a girl that could do that, Nance," Howard said. Nance looked off in the distance at the peak of Cataloochee Mountain and chewed on her twig.

"You want to get married?" he asked her.

"I reckon," Nance said, still looking away.

"You will?"

"It'd be all right, I reckon."

Howard jumped down off the porch and his foot landed in some chicken droppings and he slid down and messed up the left leg of his Sunday pants. He got up and got between Nance's skinny legs and kissed her on the cheek.

"But I don't want you messing with me if I say no," she said.

"I won't do nothing you don't want to, Nance. I'll be

good to you. We'll work hard and have plenty. We'll have as much as Jase Ledford!"

Nance sat, quiet.

"We'll get married in the Baptist church, and we'll build us a house on my folks' place, and we'll have our own bedroom, and have some younguns, and . . . and be happy!"

Howard ran off down the Indian trail, thrilled and full of hope.

They married on a pretty morning in May, and the next day Howard, Dude Hannah and Joe Putnam—and of course Nance, too—set to work building a cabin on the Kerley land, on the eastern edge of Jonathan's Creek, right in the shadow of Utah Mountain. Zeb and Maggie Phillips didn't help with the building but contributed a generous supply of moonshine. John Conard couldn't help, either. His health was gradually declining. But he was glad for his daughter. He knew Howard Kerley was a good boy and a good match for Nance, or close to it, anyway; and he deeply hoped she would find some happiness in life.

The men and Nance would work some and drink some. And then work some more. Nance was small, about five-foot-one, but she worked like a man. And she would have a pull on the jug now and then but never show it. The weather was pretty that spring and they made good progress on the cabin. Howard and Nance continued living with their folks until it was built. By the middle of June they moved in and that night Howard made love to

Nance, clumsily and gratefully and tenderly. Nance realized it was something she was expected to put up with so she didn't struggle.

The next day she went out walking for no good reason. She started out after breakfast and walked to the foot of Utah Mountain and then started up. She walked up the side of Utah by the path that went over into town. She went over the top of the mountain and down a little way on the other side, and then sat down beside the path and looked out over Waynesville. She saw the courthouse and the stores and the fine churches. Over to her right, to the west, she could see the Ledford mansion and its old slave quarters.

She couldn't help thinking about Jase, but the thought just amounted to a sad and empty feeling. She knew she could have been a help to Jase but she was too poor and that was that. Jase would find a rich girl. That was how things worked.

Through the trees she noticed a patch of pretty, pale blue wildflowers. She pushed through the weeds and bushes and made her way over toward them. They were growing on the side of a rock cliff that stuck out four or five feet. As she crept out onto the ledge she saw there was a little cave behind the flowers, a cleft in the rock that went about four feet back. A good place for snakes, she thought, and shivered. She crouched down and picked the flowers quickly. They would look pretty on the window sill in her new kitchen. She almost smiled.

She made her way back to the trail and walked slowly

toward home, toward her new house and her new husband. She intended to be as good a wife to Howard as she could manage, though she could not help thinking him a fool for loving her, for putting his boyish heart into her cold hands.

———

Nance turned twenty-one in 1869. One Sunday in the summer of that year Jase Ledford sat alone in the back pew of Jonathan's Creek Baptist Church and watched her, her thin arms and lovely sullen face, and it hit him just how much he loved her and wanted her.

The congregation sang "Jesus, I Come" as the preacher invited the repentant to come to the altar and kneel and get right with God. And of course Mrs. Shirley Clemmons came and knelt, as she did every other Sunday, and everyone except Jase waited expectantly for Shirley's confession and witness, which were always stimulating.

Jase was remembering a bright day when he was six and Nance was nine, how they goosed each other's ribs and fell and tumbled over and over in the tall grass behind the mansion, how her brown hair fell across his face when she held him down, her skinny crotch rubbing against him and snot coming out her nose as she laughed.

Shirley Clemmons, who was fat, nasty and loud, was now confessing to walking the streets of Waynesville, doing secret, evil things with drunken men for money, sliding toward hell but saved again, praise Jesus, saved again. Some in the congregation shook their heads and some wept and some prayed and gave thanks. And some chuckled.

Jase recalled the time when Nance got him behind the big oak tree beside the pasture and said, "Look here," and pulled her dress up—a blue dress with white polka dots—and pulled her bloomers down and then back up real fast, too fast for him to see anything. "Now you," she had said, with an eager, wicked look on her face.

"No!" Jase had said, and tried to run away, but she caught him and pulled his britches down and looked, and he cried.

"Crybaby!" she had said. "If you tell on me I'll put a damn hex on you. I'll make your thing shrivel up and fall off."

He had never told anyone, and he had never trusted her after that. He had decided she was a bad girl. But he had always loved her, and always would.

Streaks of rain began to hit the windowpanes of the little church. The testimony over, the parishioners were filing out, smiling and patting one another's shoulders and shaking one another's hands.

When Nance and Howard came past him Jase could see that Nance was pregnant. He watched her eyes and they rose to meet his, unabashed, unashamed. She looked through him and a wave of anger washed over him. It wasn't fair. He had lost everyone he loved. He had nobody.

He was the last to leave the church and at the door the

preacher shook his hand. "Good to see you again, Jase," he said. "But tell me, when you going to find you a little girl to spark?"

Jase laughed good-naturedly. "Don't know. One of these days." His eyes were on Nance, who was climbing up beside her husband into their wagon.

In December 1869 Nance bore Howard Kerley a son, Woodrow, with big ears and a happy disposition like his father's. When the boy was nearly seven, in November 1876, Nance's father finally died, so her mother sold their house and land to Jase Ledford and took weak-minded Elmer across Cataloochee Mountain into Tennessee, where she had a sister, Mary Ann.

"You take care of yourself and Howard and little Woody," Kathleen told Nance when they left. Nance said nothing, didn't even wave as the wagon rolled away. That was the last time she saw her mother.

So then Nance was left with nobody but Howard and the boy. Howard was a fair husband and a good father, but poor, of course; and he sometimes went on with foolishness, which Nance didn't abide. He never gave up trying to get a laugh or a smile out of Nance, though he never had any luck.

By 1882 Nance and Howard had been married sixteen years. Woody, now almost thirteen, was a pleasant, out-going, good-hearted boy, and he loved music. He loved to play the harmonica. Nance did her wifely duty by Howard once in a while, but she didn't enjoy it; she lay still like a dead person and put up with it and tried not to think about it.

But she cared for Howard, as much as her poor, miserable heart would allow. She cooked and cleaned and cut weeds and hoed potatoes and canned and sewed and plowed and knitted and quilted. Her life, though perhaps not happy, was full. When she had time to think, in the few minutes between work and sleep, her mind sometimes wandered and stumbled upon a memory of Jase Ledford.

One night near Christmas 1882 Howard woke up and Woody was there beside him but not Nance. He got up and walked quietly through the house, which was dark and cold except for some embers in the fireplace. Through a window he saw her standing in the moonlight outside the back door, under the bare maple tree. Her arms were folded over her breasts and she was looking into the woods. There was a rime of frost over everything and the world and Nance looked utterly beautiful to Howard. It was a moment he remembered until he died.

She was looking into the darkness of the woods as if she were waiting for someone. Actually she was remembering a Christmas when she was five and her father brought her a box of stick candy from young Zeb Phillips's store. It was striped peppermint and looked so wonderful and tasted so good. But that was in that happy fairyland of childhood, the land of Turnip-top, before the bear got Elmer.

The memory of the bear always made her flinch and

hurt inside. She turned from the dark, awful, beautiful woods and looked up into the cold, crisp December sky, at the stars so clear and bright. She traced the seven stars of the big water dipper her father had shown her one cold night many years ago. Tears came to her eyes.

"Nance?" Howard said.

She wiped her eyes and looked around. "Couldn't sleep," she said. Her breath condensed into a fog.

Howard looked up at the stars and wondered what was eating at Nance. He couldn't figure it out and he knew very well that Nance wouldn't say, so he went into the house and back to bed. After a while Nance did, too.

Chapter Four

In November of the next year, 1883, Jase Ledford was
riding home from Waynesville and met Nance walking
the other way, toward town. She was carrying a broken
ax.

"Good afternoon, Nance," he said, stopping his horse.
Nance shielded her eyes from the midday sun. She still
had her looks, Jase noted, though she was thirty-five
now. She had a birch twig stuck between her teeth.

"Ax broke," she said.

"Want a ride?" he asked.

"I reckon not. I like to walk."

"You and your family making out all right?"

"Reckon so." She folded her arms over her breasts and looked at him.

"Still see you in church every Sunday."

"Yep," she said. She had a sun grin on her face and almost looked as if she were laughing at him.

"See you, Nance," he said. He goosed his horse's sides and rode on, and Nance walked toward town.

When Jase got home he went to the oak cabinet that Dude Hannah had made for him and took out a quart jar of clear, pure moonshine he had bought from Zeb Phillips. He took a big drink of the stuff, and then another, and then paused to get his breath back. He went out onto the big front porch and sat down and let the old, familiar woozy feeling wash through him as he wondered why he had such a yearning for Nance Conard. Kerley.

He had once believed that there was a woman for every man. His mother had told him that. A woman for every man, like his mother for his father. He took another swallow of the corn liquor and felt the old grief and loneliness bite into him and in his dolorous state he let himself go and tears rolled down onto his shaggy mustache. He had nothing and nobody but the farm, the most prosperous farm in Haywood County but still just a *thing*, a bunch of *things*, not a person.

He wanted somebody. He wanted Nance. He admitted

it to himself. His mother had been reburied after the war and his folks, both of them, lay now in the churchyard of Jonathan's Creek Baptist Church. They at least had each other. They were not alone.

He left the porch and walked down the Indian trail to the churchyard and walked among the gravestones: Phillips, McCracken, Jones, Hatley, Conard, Ledford. His mother and father were laid beside each other with a space in between for him. The gravestones said,

Maj. William Ledford	Emily Caldwell Ledford
b. Oct. 1, 1826 d. Oct. 12, 1865	b. Feb. 3, 1832 d. Feb. 5, 1865
Loving Husband and Father	Loving Wife and Mother

He imagined his own would say,

Jason Robert Ledford
b. Mar. 9, 1850 d. ?
Son

Just "son," nothing more. He fell to his knees and sobbed and dug his fingers into the dead grass.

After a while he looked up and wiped his eyes. The episode was easing off. He looked up past the gravestones, past the little church, through the bare maple trees, at the meandering Indian trail that disappeared into the woods. He knew where Nance's true soul dwelt— it was in the cold, dark forest, among the shadows of the maple, birch, oak and sycamore, beneath the moss, among the unseen leaves.

Howard was out by the smokehouse sitting on a stump, whittling, when Nance got home with the new ax. Woody was sitting on the back porch steps playing his harmonica. Nance handed the ax to Howard and he admired it.

"Going to need firewood tonight," he said, and eyed the woods, trying to pick out a likely tree.

"Hog-killing time," Nance said. "Moon's on the wane."

"I can kill it," Howard said. "But I ain't no good at cutting it up. I get them little pieces of bone all in the meat."

"Dude Hannah's the best at that, on Jonathan's Creek," Woody said.

"I reckon so," Howard said. "And he's a good old boy. But I kind of hate to fool with him. Always going on with some foolishness."

"He can cut up a hog," Nance said.

"I'll ride over tomorrow and see if he can do it," Howard said.

Woody was blowing "Good-bye, Sweet Liza Jane" on his harmonica. He had dark hair like Nance and was gangly and simple like Howard.

The next day Howard rode across the back side of Cataloochee Mountain to Dude Hannah's cabin. It was evening and Dude was sitting on a stool on his front porch working on an oak cabinet, sanding it. There was a jug of Zeb Phillips's moonshine beside him.

"Hey there, Dude!" Howard hollered.

Dude looked up and grinned. "Howard! Good to see you. Keeping that family walking the chalk line?"

"They're doing fine. We need our hog killed and cut up."

"Sure, sure," Dude said, lighting a cigarette. "Good time. Moon's on the wane. Be glad to help you out."

"We'll pay you."

"Just a little pork meat and some shortnin' bread, that's all I need. Love my pork meat, yes sir!"

"Tomorrow morning?" He knew Dude was trying to be funny so he grinned a lame grin. He really didn't like Dude much.

"You heat up the water. I'll bring the implements. I'll be there after I've drunk my coffee, tomorrow morning."

"That's fine," Howard said, and rode off toward home. Dude had never acted just right since he came home from the war, Howard thought. There was a look about him as if he were about to play a trick on you.

Dude showed up at the Kerleys' little cabin early the next morning in his wagon. He climbed over into the back of the wagon and picked up a big lard bucket full of killing and carving tools and a twenty-foot length of rope and climbed down. Nance and Woody came out to meet him, with Howard behind them.

"Around back," Howard said, and they all four walked around behind the house. There was a chicken coop with about twenty fat, white Plymouth Rocks, and the smokehouse, and the outhouse, and the hog lot. Beside the hog lot was a large, black cast-iron pot full of water with a wood fire burning under it. Beside the smokehouse was a makeshift table—some boards laid across two sawhorses. Just behind the smokehouse, close to the woods, was a maple tree with one low-hanging limb.

"That'un?" Dude asked, pointing to a big old boar.

"Old Dandy, that's him," Howard said.

Nance had her arms folded and a birch twig in her mouth. Woody had his hands stuck down into his overalls pockets. He liked the old hog but he had always known what its destiny would be. He knew some life had to be sacrificed for other life to go on. He started whistling "Wildwood Flower" but Dude looked at him and he hushed and then they all stood looking at each other for a minute.

"Let's get on with it," Dude said, and Howard could smell the liquor on his breath. Dude dropped his rope and set his lard bucket down in the dirt and the tools in it rattled. He reached into it and brought out a Smith & Wesson .45 revolver and got two cartridges and loaded them into the gun. He went to the hogpen and aimed at Dandy and fired once. A hole appeared two inches up from the hog's right eye and it dropped like a boulder.

Dude looked around at Nance and grinned and winked. He took the other cartridge out of the pistol and put it into his pocket and then put the pistol back into the bucket. Then he took out a huge bowie knife and straddled the hog and pulled its snout up and ripped the knife across its throat and dug it down deep into its heart.

Blood spurted out at Nance and the others in gouts. "Whoo-ee, old piggy! Better watch out!" Dude hollered much too late, and laughed gleefully. There was blood all over Nance's dress and Howard's overalls and Woody's dirty bare feet.

They let it bleed a few minutes and then the two men carried it over to the pot and lowered it headfirst by its legs into the scalding water. In a minute they pulled it up and lowered the other end, and then the front end again, and so on, over and over, and every once in a while Dude would yank at some bristles, and they'd lower it again, over and over until finally a tuft of the hog's hair came out in Dude's fingers.

"Here he comes! Ol' piggy's ready!" Dude hollered, and he and Howard pulled the hog out of the water and laid it on the table and started furiously pulling and scraping the hair off before it could set. "Got to get that hair off before it sets," Dude said. "If it sets you can't get it out no which way." Howard knew that but he held his peace and kept scraping and pulling.

When the hair was pretty well cleaned off Dude got his rope and tied it around the hog's hind legs and threw the other end of the rope across the low-hanging limb of the maple tree. Then he and Howard hoisted the hog up and tied the rope around the trunk of the tree. Dude slit the hog's belly and gutted it and then they all threw buckets of water onto the carcass to wash it out. Then they let it hang and drain.

Dude lit a cigarette and sat down on a stump. He was bloody all over and his eyes were narrow and black and shiny and he was grinning. Nance could tell he was watching her and she folded her arms and leaned against the side of the house and looked down at her wet dress and bloody shoes.

The sun had nearly reached its zenith but the November air was cold. Dude went to his wagon and brought back his jug and passed it around. Woody got out his harmonica and played "Cripple Creek" and they started dancing and singing and laughing, except Nance, though later she did drink some and dance a little. Dude got very loud and raucous and Howard considered telling him to quiet down, but there was no good reason to. The nearest house was the Putnams', three miles down the Indian trail.

After they all grew tired Nance went into the house to start cooking. Dude and Howard sat down on the steps of the smokehouse.

"You know Zeb Phillips's boy, little Birch?" Dude asked. "He ain't but four years old, and already Zeb's got him a-working at that still. One day I went up in that holler behind the store, and there that little blondheaded feller was, dragging limbs up and throwing them on the fire."

"Zeb and Maggie never figured on having kids,"

Howard said. "Zeb's fifty now, and Maggie's no spring chicken."

"Remember old Father Abraham," Dude said.

"You don't go to church, Dude," Howard chided. "How'd you come to know about Father Abraham?"

"I used to go, when I was a kid," he said, his face clouding over. He took a big swallow of liquor, and then another, and then laughed and jumped up and started buck-dancing around in the dirt as Woody played "Turkey in the Straw."

In the kitchen Nance was stirring up cornmeal and water to make fritter cakes. Outside Woody started playing a slow, sweet version of "Wildwood Flower," and Nance sang softly, almost in a whisper, just to herself:

I will twine and will mingle my raven-black hair,
With the roses so red and the lilies so fair,
The myrtle so bright with its emerald hue,
And a pale wildwood flower with petals light blue.

Oh, he taught me to love him, he promised to love
And to cherish me always all others above.
I woke from my dream and my idol was clay,
All my passion for loving had vanished away.

I will dance, I will sing and my life will be gay,
I will banish this weeping, drive troubles away.
I will live yet to see him regret this dark hour
When he won and neglected this frail wildwood flower.

She looked up and Dude was standing just inside the back door, looking at her. His shirt was open and his hard, brown stomach glistened with sweat and there were dried, rusty streaks of hog's blood on his arms and chest.

"Nice big'un," he said.

"Yep," Nance said, stirring hard at her mixing bowl. She glanced up at him and he grinned his wicked smile and she looked away quickly. Through the kitchen window she could see Howard hopping and dancing near the smokehouse, swinging Dude's jug.

"Keep you in eats till Christmas," Dude said, rubbing his belly.

"We're much obliged." She whacked several more times at the fritter mix and then set it down. She went to the big oak kitchen cabinet that Dude had made them and took out a bucket of lard and dug her fingers into it and slapped a little gob into a big black fry-pan and set the pan on the stove. In a few minutes the lard began to swirl and melt. Outside she could hear Woody playing "Black Jack Davy" on his harmonica. She took the corn-meal mix and poured it into the fry-pan in four puddles and it sizzled and smoked. Then she felt Dude's hand on her back.

"Ever go down to the mill anymore, Nance?" he asked. She felt his warm whiskey breath.

"No. Not in a long time." He smelled like the hog's blood, like some dangerous animal. Nance stepped away and set the bowl down and then went into the small pantry at the corner of the kitchen and reached into a burlap sack and got four potatoes. She laid them on the table and got her butcher knife down from a rack on the wall that Dude had also made. The knife was sharpened down to half its original width. She looked at Dude again, at his shiny black eyes.

"I aim to go there tomorrow. Right after supper," he said.

At that moment Howard came in the back door. He looked at each of them and wiped his nose with the back of his hand. "How long till we eat, Nance?"

"Won't be too long," she said, and started peeling the potatoes over a slop bucket beside the table.

Outside Woody was playing "Maple on the Hill." Howard went back out into the yard. Dude caught Nance's eye and winked and went outside, too. Nance noticed her hands were trembling and discovered she had cut her thumb and was bleeding all over the potato she was trying to peel.

After they had their meal Howard and Dude lowered the hog from the tree and hefted it up onto the sawhorse table. It took Dude a couple of hours to cut it up properly and then they took the meat and salted it down and laid it in the smokehouse. Dude saved out a portion of pork meat for himself and Nance put it into a washtub for him and he gathered up his tools and climbed into his wagon.

"Now you remember old Dude when you're eating that pork meat," he said, and rode off. Howard and Woody waved at him as he left. Nance just stood with her arms folded and the stem of a maple leaf in her mouth.

The next evening Woody lay dozing on his bed and Howard was out back while Nance washed the supper dishes. When she was finished she went to the back door and stood looking out. Everything was quiet and so she took off her apron and slipped out the door and hurried down toward the woods behind the house.

As he was coming out of the smokehouse Howard saw her enter the woods. When he got to the house he went to the kitchen and looked out the back door and found Nance's apron on the steps. He picked it up and folded it the way she usually did and then stood looking out toward the woods, scratching his head.

Nance pushed her way through the bushes and over the thick bed of dead leaves and finally she came out on the bank of Jonathan's Creek. She walked along the creek bank for half a mile and came to the place where the old mill stood.

The mill had been powered by an overshot water wheel that no longer turned. It was decayed and covered with moss, a sad and beautiful thing to Nance. She had played here with Jase and Elmer and Jane when she was a girl, and sometimes with Dude, too. The mill had been used to grind corn and wheat before the war but the man who owned it was a Union sympathizer and he had sold all his property—mill, cabin and all—to William Ledford. After the war Jase let it go to ruin.

Nance sat on the bank and stuck a long blade of dry

grass in her mouth. There was a sweet autumn chill and she shivered and folded her arms over her breasts and waited. In a few minutes she heard a rustling in the bushes across the creek and Dude appeared.

He hopped lightly across the creek on four or five big rocks and sat down beside Nance, grinning his familiar, wicked grin. "Hey there, old girl," he said. She looked at him without smiling.

"This old mill's been here since 1790, my daddy told me," Dude said.

"It ain't turned in a long time," Nance said.

"A man got killed here. A feller name of Jonathan McElroy. I reckon it's him the creek was named after. Him and his brother and some other men was after some Indians and he got killed, and they didn't have time to bury him proper. So they laid him in the creek to keep animals from getting to him, I reckon, or to keep him from rottening. But when they got back he was gone."

"A bear," Nance said.

"Could of been," Dude said. "Reckon I could get that wheel to turning again?"

"Too old," Nance said. "It wouldn't hold up."

Dude got up and went behind the big water wheel and climbed up on it. He moved the trough so it would catch water and spill it on the wheel. The wheel creaked and moaned and then weaved as if it were about to topple.

Nance jumped up, her eyes big. "It's gonna fall!"

But it slowly began to turn. Dude grinned and came over to Nance and put his hands gently on her arms and said, "Reckon I could get your old wheels a-turning again, Nance?"

She took the blade of grass out of her mouth and put her fists up to his chest as if to push him away but he pulled her close and bent down and kissed her. Her arms went around his neck and held him tightly and at that moment they heard noise in the woods and Howard stepped out, and then Woody behind him.

"What are you all a-doing out here in the woods?" Howard asked. All four stood in silence on the creek bank. The sun was going down and somewhere nearby a screech owl cried.

Finally Howard spoke again: "You'll have to get out, Nance." Woody looked away and stuck his hands into his overalls pockets and tried to whistle but couldn't. Nance reached down and pulled up another blade of grass and stuck it between her teeth and folded her arms and looked down at her worn-out shoes. Howard turned and went back through the woods toward the house and Woody followed him.

Dude stood for a minute, his hands on his hips. He wiped his nose with his knuckles and looked at Nance and grinned. "Reckon you'll need a place to stay," he said.

So Nance left Howard and Woody and moved into Dude's lonely, dark little cabin, which hadn't felt a woman's touch in almost twenty years. She wiped away the dust and mold that covered everything except Dude's boots and guns. She took the hides off the wall and got up some of the caked mud off the floor and put up some new curtains in place of the old ones, which were rotted and torn to shreds.

In October 1884 she had a baby girl and named her Elizabeth Ann. Dude was in the Waynesville jail when his daughter was born and didn't care what she was named or even whether she was born at all. Nance had to have her alone, with no help. Or anyway she didn't ask anyone for help. She reasoned that she'd made her own bed and ought to lie in it.

Dude didn't change. He could do anything, fix anything. He could build an oak cabinet or a bookshelf or a bed, or repair a fence or a roof or a tool or a gun, or butcher a hog or a cow or a deer, and if he didn't know how to do something right off he would figure it out. And people would pay him well. But then he would go to Waynesville, to Dillard's Bar, and get drunk and lose the money gambling or get it stolen. Then he would stagger home and curse Nance and slap her around. And as little Lizzy got older he would hit her, too. He had no patience with women.

Still everyone was inclined to say that Dude was a good old boy. He was generous and helpful to everybody, which kept him away from home and left most of the work to Nance—plowing, hoeing corn and chopping wood, along with the housework.

But Nance never complained; and as Lizzy grew she was able to help with some of the chores. By the time she was six she could mop and sweep and wash clothes, and Nance would set her up on the plow to hold it down so it would dig deeper into the earth. But as hard as they worked they were still just womenfolk, and the crops would usually turn out scant.

The people of Jonathan's Creek were not as understanding of Nance as they were of Dude. They talked about her leaving a good, honest man like Howard Kerley for a hell-raiser like Dude Hannah, and what was worse, leaving her son, not to mention having a child by Dude out of wedlock. Most concluded that she was sorry and no-good, and that she was getting no worse than she deserved. They wouldn't sit on the same bench with her at church, and when Lizzy started school the other children would call her "Dude Hannah's bastard" and tell her that her mother was "Dude Hannah's whore."

But Nance endured.

Chapter Five

They all grew older, as people do. At the time of the county fair of 1890, where he met Lucille Frady, Jase Ledford was forty.

It was the middle of October and the leaves of the trees along the road to Waynesville were a flaming fire of colors—beautiful, though to Jase they were harbingers of age and decay.

Forty. How could he have got so old? His father was just thirty-nine when he died. His mother was thirty-three. He still felt the pain their loss had caused him, the loneliness of the years of trying to build back the farm. It was as if all he had ever felt was pain and loss and loneliness.

He still thought about Nance and felt a deep anger at her, though he knew it wasn't her fault that he had been too young, too well-to-do, too stupid and slow. But he couldn't forgive her for leaving a good man like Howard Kerley for a hard-drinking rascal like Dude Hannah. If he'd realized she wasn't happy with Howard, well, he just might have done something. As it was now he felt he'd lost her twice.

His wagon ran over a rock and his hogs grunted. He felt just like them, like another prize hog, and in fact he was fat now. He weighed a good two hundred pounds. Eating well was one luxury he allowed himself, and besides, being fat was quite in keeping with the image of the prosperous farmer. And he was no longer interested in impressing the womenfolk. He had said to hell with them long ago.

About halfway to town he met the new Baptist preacher, the Reverend Colby Rabb. Rabb was a thin, pale man—an overgrown boy, really—with a toothbrush mustache and a sneaky look, like a weasel. But he had a wife and three kids.

"Taking them hogs to the fair?" the preacher asked as they pulled alongside each other. "Mighty fine specimens."

"Yes sir," Jase said. "You been?"

"Just coming back. Lots of fine-looking animals. Mr. J. D. Roberts brought his Arabian horses. Beautiful animals, they shore are. Bill McClure's there with his Black Angus bull, and J. D. Hatley with his big old Plymouth Rock chickens. Great big fat ones. And A. T. Frady's got two of his Hereford cows. And his daughter, Lucille." He winked at Jase.

"Livestock of all kinds," Jase said.

"That Lucille shore is a pretty girl, Jase. She shore is. And there's nobody good enough for her around here, what with A. T.'s position and all."

Jase grinned. "Too old to think about such things, Reverend. You trying to drum you up some business?"

"Naw, naw. The Fradys are Presbyterians anyway. Just showing some concern for your soul. I don't think a single man has got much of a chance of going to heaven, I shore don't. And Ecclesiastes tells us, 'Whoso getteth a wife getteth a good thing.' And I hold by that."

Jase laughed amiably, tipped his hat to the preacher and rode on. He felt sour. He was old enough to be the preacher's father, old enough to be a grandfather. It was as if he'd been cursed.

Most of the farmers in the county were at the fair. Jase put his two sleek, beautiful Hampshires in a stall beside the other hogs and meandered around, just looking. He struck up a conversation with Bill McClure near the cattle stalls. Bill jabbered about how much he'd paid for his bull and how well he treated it, on and on. A few yards away was A. T. Frady, talking with J. D. Roberts. Frady's daughter, Lucille, looked around with a bored, spiteful look.

Their eyes met but Lucille looked at him as if he didn't exist. Jase had known her, or of her, since she was a girl. He didn't know her very well, didn't want to. It was plain that she was spoiled and smart-alecky. She had not married, though she was twenty-nine, for the simple reason that nobody could have outdone her father in babying her—that and the fact that A. T. considered his daughter too good for any of the hillbillies in Waynesville. Though of course he was one himself.

"Look, Daddy," Lucille said. "There's Jase Ledford." She always enjoyed pointing out men more prosperous than her father; it gave her leverage in getting whatever she wanted. Not that she needed it. She was A. T.'s only child.

"So it is," A. T. said. "Let's go say hello." He led Lucille over to Jase and shook his hand. "Jase, and Bill! You both know my daughter, Lucille."

"Hello, Lucille," Jase said. "Come to the fair with your daddy?"

"Well, I suppose anyone could see that. I told Daddy I didn't care to come but he insisted and so I wore this old thing and . . ."

"Looks good," Bill McClure said. He was a bit

flustered because he hadn't gotten to the good part about his bull. Like everyone who knew Lucille he knew that the only way to get a word in was to interrupt. Lucille had a way of ending everything she said with "and" or "but" and chattering right on.

"Bring your Herefords?" Jase asked A. T.

"Sure did," A. T. said, and turned to point at them, which gave Lucille another opening.

"I can't understand how all these grown men can get *so* worked up over a bunch of nasty animals but that's *all* that happens around here. I *do* wish there was a nice dance or something so a body could get really dressed up and look nice and see some men wearing clean clothes instead of dirty overalls and . . ."

"Like in the big city?" Jase asked, smiling. Somehow there was something about her—her frown?—that he almost liked.

"Yes," she said. "It's been the longest time since we had a party. Daddy's so busy with his responsibilities as representative, and I know it's important and all, but . . ."

"Maybe we can get somebody to throw a party," Jase said. Bill McClure was looking around for someone to listen to his story about his bull.

"Yes. I was saying Daddy's crops didn't do too well this fall," Lucille went on, "and taxes are up, and he's promised me a new saddle and riding outfit, and . . ."

"I'll bet you look real pretty in a riding outfit," Jase said. He realized he was trying to flirt.

"Why, would you like to come to the farm tomorrow?" Lucille ventured, and A. T. beamed. A. T. was a cheerful man, like his brother, Henry, who ran the funeral home in Waynesville. He was pleased—and surprised—at Lucille's interest in Jase. Jase was not just another hillbilly. He was rich.

Four months later A. T. Frady dropped dead across the barbed-wire fence that encircled his expensive cattle. He was fifty-nine. Jase married Lucille a month after that. Then in 1892, in February, they had a son, Andrew William. Jase was so proud of his son, and so busy trying to keep Lucille happy, that he almost forgot about Nance. But the truth was that Nance had left an emptiness in him that nothing could completely fill.

Still he felt a level of joy that he had come to believe was impossible for him, and he was grateful, even though Lucille was an awful bore, and lazy and spiteful and greedy by nature. And then a year later she presented him with little Joellen, and he could no longer deny, even to himself, that he was happy. The children—especially the boy—gave meaning to his days and set him looking toward the future. He cherished them.

The same year Joellen Ledford was born, 1893, Jane Putnam, Nance's childhood friend, gave birth to a son, William. Nobody knew how old Jane was but they all knew she was Nance's age at least. She'd suffered five or six stillbirths since the war and she and Joe had given up hoping for children. But the boy was healthy.

Jase took little notice but Lucille griped about it for a month. "Just one more hungry mouth to feed, that's what it amounts to," she said. "They don't pay any rent. They're living off our charity. The old man is too puny to work and help. I say we charge them rent, or make them move off our land."

And so on.

Chapter Six

On a cold day in December 1896 Nance was standing looking out the kitchen window with her arms folded and a birch twig in her mouth, wondering what she could fix for supper. There was a little canned pork but no beef, not much cornmeal and no flour. They'd have to buy some provisions, which meant she'd have to ask Dude for money.

Lizzy sat on the floor next to the fireplace trying to read her history book. She was twelve and in the sixth grade, which was as far as school went in those days.

"You know about the Alamo, Mama?"

"Don't reckon I ever heard of that," Nance said.

"It was a fort down in Texas. A little bunch of men held off a thousand Mexicans there in 1836."

"I wasn't born till 1848."

"How far back can you recall, Mama? Do you remember the Civil War? Miss Cordelia says we'll take that up next."

"Yep," Nance said. "Them was hard times."

Dude came riding up and dismounted and stomped into the house. "Damn!" he said, rubbing his hands together. He was drunk as usual but he was grinning about something. Nance and Lizzy were relieved to see him in a good mood.

"Mighty cold," he said, and clomped over to the fireplace and turned his back to the fire, still grinning and watching Nance and Lizzy; and they were watching him.

"Come here," he said to Lizzy, and she got up and went to him cautiously. "Hold out your hand," he said, and she did. Wrinkles appeared in her brow and tears began to form in her eyes. She was afraid of him.

"Here," Dude said, and handed her a silver dollar. Lizzy took the coin and turned it over and over. Her eyes sparkled and she looked up at her father. "Does old Dude get a kiss?" he asked.

Lizzy stood on her tiptoes and kissed his bearded cheek. "Can I really spend it?" she asked.

"You run down to Zeb's store and buy whatever you damn please," he said. Then Dude winked at Nance.

"Come here, Nance, old girl." He held out his hand, in which there were four more silver dollars. With his other arm he pulled Nance close to him and kissed her.

"This will help out," Nance said. "We need flour and sugar and some meat. And hog feed and chicken feed."

"Tomorrow you go and get whatever you need. What have we got for tonight?"

"We ain't got but seven chickens left," Nance said, holding the coins up to look at them more closely.

"Cook one. We'll buy us some more," Dude said, grinning. "You know the Marcus woman, whose boy shot her? I built the casket and dug the grave, and I carved the name on the headstone. Frady's Funeral Home would have charged that boy thirty or forty dollars, and I done it all for five. I told him I couldn't do no embalming or nothing like that, but he said it weren't necessary."

Nance nodded.

"Go on," Dude said to Lizzy, and she ran out the door and down the Indian trail toward Zeb Phillips's store, love for her father brimming over in her heart. The air was very cold and the afternoon sky was brownish gray and she could tell there was snow coming.

It was three miles to the store and she was chilled to the bone when she got there. She opened the door gently and gradually and peeked in, not wanting to take it all in at once, wanting to savor it.

"Hey, Lizzy!" Birch Phillips hollered at her from behind the big counter. He was Zeb and Maggie's boy, now seventeen.

"Hello, Birch. Merry Christmas!"

"Merry Christmas to you. What's Santa Claus going to bring you?"

"I'm twelve, Birch. You know I don't believe in such stuff no more."

"Why, I reckon you're a regular old lady," he teased. She didn't like it, coming from Birch, because she had a secret liking for him. "Reckon you'll be getting married before long," he said.

"There ain't nobody on Jonathan's Creek I'd have as a husband. Specially not you."

"Me? Lord, I believe you've done and broke my heart! But I ain't fixing to get married. I plan to wait till I'm forty, like old Jase Ledford. I'm too young to die yet."

She went past the dry goods and savored each smell: hemp rope, stiff-starched overalls and union suits, rubber boots, leather shoes and harnesses and straps, gun oil, coal oil, wool blankets, bolts of gingham, percale and calico. And then she came to the foodstuffs: hoop cheese, dill pickles, bacon, ham, sacks of flour, coffee, molasses, cinnamon sticks. And then the chicken feed, hog feed and dairy feed. And over it all, stirring up all the aromas and blending with them, was the smell of the hickory and pine and balsam burning in the old potbellied wood stove. It was glorious, wonderful, a moment she would remember all her life. She had a dollar, and she thought she might go crazy and start crying for joy.

But she contained herself. "I want a dollar's worth of something," she said.

"You got a dollar to spend?"

"On whatever I damn please."

"Ain't you uppity! Who give you a dollar?"

"My daddy."

"Well, I wouldn't trust you with a dollar, I don't think. You're too swimmy-headed."

"I'm not. I got plenty of sense, Miss Cordelia says. She says I got promise."

"Promise? To do what?"

"I'm good at reading and writing."

"Women need to be pretty and sweet, so they can catch a man."

"I don't need no man," Lizzy said.

"Well, what will it be?" Birch asked after a pause.

She closed her eyes, pointed her finger and twirled. When she stopped she was pointing to a horse collar. She winced and glanced at Birch and he laughed. "Too big?" he asked, and she laughed, too.

"Look here," he said, holding up a little twig with green leaves and white berries. "You know what this is?"

She held her breath and put her finger up to her lips. "Mistletoe."

"You got to kiss me," he said.

"I don't kiss no boys," she said, watching his eyes and twisting back and forth.

"You got to," Birch said, and came out from behind the counter after her. She squealed and ran behind the overalls with Birch right behind her. She turned to face him and backed up against the big sacks of hog feed, giggling wildly as Birch drew closer and closer. She quit giggling as he held the mistletoe overhead. "You got to," he said again. She looked into his eyes and saw them sweep over her, taking her all in. She let her lips part to meet his and she felt weak at his touch, he was so tender. Her hands went up to his shoulders, wanting to hold him.

But then he backed away and there was something like fear or surprise on his face. Then he grinned and took the mistletoe away, as if it were all just a joke. "Now then, how do you plan to spend that fortune you got?" he asked, and went back behind the counter.

She realized she was on her tiptoes and her back was still up against the hog feed. She sighed involuntarily and swallowed. Getting control of herself, she twirled again. "I want some of everything, everything!" she said. Then she saw, on the shelf behind Birch, a pretty baby doll with big blue eyes and a coy smile. It seemed to capture all the happiness she felt. "*That's* what I want," she said. "How much is it?"

"Uh, well," Birch said, and looked at the doll. "It's a dollar and a half. It's imported from Germany."

"Oh, well, that's okay." She picked out a box of stick candy and some cheese and crackers and a bar of perfumed soap and two pairs of red socks and set them all down on the counter, and Birch added them up on a piece of a paper bag. As he calculated he saw Lizzy's eyes shift longingly back to the doll behind him, but he pretended not to notice.

"You got thirty-two cents left," he said. "How about buying me a present?"

"You done had your present," she said, and felt her face burn. "But maybe I should get Mama and Dude something."

"Here's something Dude might like," Birch said, and from under the counter he brought out a pocketknife shaped like a dog's hind leg, with handles of gold-green bone.

"Ooh, that's pretty," she said, but then frowned. "How much is it?"

"Ten cents. And here's a nice little hand mirror for Nance, and that'll leave you five cents, to put in your bank account."

She examined the mirror. It was clean and smooth and its back and handle were made of delicately carved rosewood. Maybe Nance would like it. If she did she would go "Humph," nothing more.

"Okay," Lizzy decided, and handed the mirror back to Birch. She gave him her dollar and he opened a drawer under the counter and produced a nickel but he missed her palm with it and it dropped to the floor and rolled away. Lizzy hopped after it and stopped it with her foot and picked it up and came back to the counter. Birch wrapped some thin paper around the mirror and put it and the other items into a paper bag he had waiting.

"Merry Christmas," he said, and handed her the bag of treasures. As she reached to get it he took her hand and squeezed it gently and winked at her. Suddenly her body felt warm and loose all over and her heart crackled with love like the fire in the wood stove.

She said "Merry Christmas" and slipped out the door into the cold and dark December evening. There was a halo around the moon and the stars were huge and bright and clear. She sang Christmas songs all the way home and almost felt guilty about being so happy. She tried to think of the true meaning of Christmas that the Reverend Rabb had spoken of, the sweet Christ child in the manger, but it was no use; all she could think of was her own private joy.

When she got home Dude and Nance were already in bed, but they'd left a lamp burning on the kitchen table and beside the lamp Nance had left her a plate of chicken and mashed potatoes and gravy. She sat at the table and ate a little and reached into the bag and took out the mirror and the jackknife, and then she realized the bag was too full for what she had bought. She dug down past the soap and the cheese and crackers and pulled out the baby doll.

She looked at it, so lovely, sweet and innocent, a perfect gift for a child. A wave of melancholy swept through her, for she knew that the child was somehow gone forever, banished to the past by a kiss.

She left the other things on the table and put out the light and took the doll with her to her cot beside Dude and Nance's bed. She held it close, her heart full and her eyes wide in the darkness, feeling the pure wonder of life—how it would give you something precious and, in the same moment, take something precious away.

On a pretty morning in April 1901 Jase Ledford un-hitched his plow horse from a wagon of manure that he and Billy intended to spread on the tomato patch. He called Andrew to take the horse to the barn.

Andrew, who was nine now, came obediently from the cornfield, where he was pulling up cornstalks. He held the singletree up as the old horse walked along, and Jase and Billy started shoveling the manure out of the wagon and onto the field. Then Andrew got the notion to set the singletree down and let it drag. Then he stepped onto it. The sudden pull of his weight spooked the ordinarily gentle old horse and it jumped and ran. Andrew fell, his foot hung between the singletree and the reins.

Jase looked up from his work to see his only son being dragged all the way to the barn, over the rocks and clumps of dirt and cornstalks.

Billy got there first. "He's killed, Mister Jase," he said. Jase fell on his knees and looked at Andrew. The boy's head was twisted backwards and his back was bent at an impossible angle. His mouth and eyes were open and his teeth were caked with dirt. He was bloody all over.

The boy had been too timid to suit Jase, who some-times doubted whether his son would ever get over being whiny and selfish like his mother. Trembling, Jase reached out to touch him but couldn't. He stopped and looked up into the hopeless, anguished face of old Billy.

"God, God," Jase said, and sighed. He knew he was a

dead man himself. His happiness was destroyed, his life ruined.

As the years passed Birch proved to be backward in his courting of Lizzy—partly because he felt she was a bit too young to be fair game and partly because of his mother's attitude. Maggie Phillips wanted Birch to do better than Lizzy Hannah. ("Is that her *legal* name?" she would ask.) So their love smoldered but never burst into flame.

Dude kept fixing and building and drinking and raising hell, and Nance kept working as she always had and always would.

Jase Ledford descended into a depression that he treated unsuccessfully with moonshine and poker at Dillard's Bar. Lucille nagged harder and harder about his spending and his gambling losses, but he paid her less and less attention. He was hardly aware that she existed, so little did she matter to him now. And his despair blinded him to his daughter, Joellen, who was sweet and pretty and cheerful. She was hurt by his neglect, but she understood. By the time he really noticed her again she was grown.

Fire Sighted

Residents of Jonathan's Creek reported a fire in that section last night. Smoke was sighted by many people but the source remains unknown.

This has been a cold, dry winter and citizens of our county are cautioned to carefully supervise all fires inside the home and out due to the danger of house fires and forest fires.

Waynesville Clarion, February 27, 1910

Chapter Seven

"Jase Ledford was fine until that horse drug little Andrew to death," Maggie Phillips was saying to old Jane Putnam in the store. Zeb was asleep in their house, behind the store, and Birch was working at the still up on the side of the mountain. "But he ain't been right since. It just goes to show, money and possessions ain't everything."

"It's sad how he's treated Joellen," Jane said.

"That Joellen's a sweet child," Maggie said. "Smart, too. I hear she's making good grades at that college in Atlanta."

"I've heard she likes Birch," Jane said, and grinned through her wrinkled old lips. She was nearing sixty-five now. "But I've heard Birch has got eyes for Lizzy Hannah."

Maggie frowned. "Why no, he's never had no interest in that poor little bastard youngun. And I don't want him throwing his life away on that girl. You know old Nance left a good man for that crazy Dude Hannah. I don't hold with such doings."

"She's had a tough row to hoe with that Dude," Jane said, and bit off a chew of tobacco. "I've heard he whips both of them twice a week."

"You know Jase Ledford used to like Nance, till she married Howard Kerley," Maggie said. "Though I don't have no idea why. She's always been sour as a crab apple."

"That Lucille leads him a dog's life. Jase don't show his face in church no more."

"Why, he goes to that Presbyterian church in Waynesville," Maggie said.

"Not no more, from what I heard. He didn't fit in with them uppity people. And you know what I heard?"

"What?"

"I heard that Presbyterian preacher goes to Asheville once a month, where he's got another woman, that he picked up off the street."

"I declare! Was she a . . . ?"

"A harlot. A whore," Jane said, and spat into the brass spittoon beside the pickle barrel.

"Looks like they'd get rid of him," Maggie said.

"Well, I heard the reason they don't is that . . ."

At that moment the door opened and in came Nance, letting in the cold February wind.

"Nance! How you a-doing?" Jane asked.

"Got to get some eats," Nance said, not smiling.

Jane and Maggie glanced at each other as Nance looked up and down the shelves at the canned goods. She picked up the cans and looked at the prices and put them all back except for a can of peaches. She brought it to the counter and set it down and fished in her little worn-out purse for a dime and laid it beside the can.

"Is that all you want, Nance?" Maggie asked.

Nance said nothing. She had on a flimsy blue dress with polka dots and a black knitted shawl. She looked like somebody in mourning. Especially her face.

"How's old Dude a-making it, Nance?" Jane asked.

"About the same," Nance said.

"Ever hear from Woody?" Maggie asked.

"He writes to Lizzy sometimes. Says he's working with a musical band."

"How old is Lizzy now, Nance?" Jane asked.

"She's about twenty-seven," Nance answered.

"You tell her I said she'd better find her a man pretty soon, Nance. They can come in mighty handy." Jane grinned and winked at Maggie. Maggie snorted.

"I'll tell her," Nance said. She was looking at a bolt of gingham in red and green paisley, rubbing it between her fingers.

"Nothing else?" Maggie asked.

"That's all," Nance said, dropping the cloth. "You got a sack for this?"

"Sure," Maggie said, and got a paper bag from beneath the counter. She put the can of peaches in it and Nance took it and left.

Jane grinned at Maggie and they both shook their heads.

That evening Nance opened the can of peaches and poured them into a bowl in front of Dude and Lizzy.

"Is that all?" Dude asked.

"It's all we got. All I could afford to buy," Nance said.

"Shit!" Dude said. He got up from the table, knocking over his chair, and went out onto the porch and sat down in the rocking chair he had built for himself and muttered curses.

Nance sat looking at the peaches a few moments and then dipped a couple into her plate and then Lizzy did the same.

Dude hollered from the porch, "Ain't we got no chickens?"

"Just the laying hens," Nance answered.

Dude got up and came back into the house. Still standing, he grabbed a couple of peach halves and ate them with his fingers.

"Damn stupid-assed woman," he muttered. Nance looked at her peaches and said nothing. Dude got his jug out of the cupboard and took it out onto the porch and started getting drunk. Nance and Lizzy knew what was coming.

Dude hollered again from the porch, "You know how much that damn Lucille Ledford paid me to fix her smokehouse roof? Fifty cents! Fifty damn cents!" He took the two quarters out of his overalls pocket and threw them into the yard.

After a few minutes he got up and went into the house. He walked into the bedroom and got his Winchester .30-30 and went out the back door and into the woods. He took his jug along.

It was nearly dark, so as Nance washed out their plates Lizzy lit the coal-oil lamp and sat down at the table and knitted. Nance sat down across from her with her hands in her lap and a twig in her mouth.

"Daddy's a good hunter," Lizzy said.

"Not when he's drunk," Nance said. "He won't bag nothing and then he'll come back and whip us."

A couple of hours later, after dark, Dude came back. He kicked the back door open. "Hey!" he hollered. "You bitches! Hey!"

Nance and Lizzy just sat, waiting. Then the rifle fired and the coal-oil lamp exploded. The tablecloth caught fire and some places on the floor blazed up. Nance and Lizzy ran out the front door into the yard. There were spots of fire on the front of Lizzy's dress and she slapped at them frantically.

The fire in the kitchen caught the curtains ablaze and spread to the walls. After Lizzy put out the fire on her dress she saw that the house was burning. Nance stood with her arms folded, doing nothing. Lizzy ran back into the house. The kitchen was a furnace now and the fire had spread to the living room. She ran into the bedroom and grabbed some clothes and Nance's old chest of things. She hooked her arm through the spinning wheel and tried to get through the front door with all of it but couldn't. She could hear her father laughing wildly and then he fired again and she heard the bullet thunk into the wall near her head.

"Stop, Daddy!" she hollered, crying. "Please stop!" She set the spinning wheel down and got the chest and the clothes out and into the yard. Nance just stood and watched.

Lizzy went back for the spinning wheel and now the whole house was afire. As she came off the porch with the spinning wheel she fell over it and broke it. She sobbed and cursed, furious at Dude and at Nance and at herself. She picked herself up and looked back at the house, which was now a huge bonfire. It was almost beautiful.

Dude staggered around to where the women were and watched the fire with them, grinning crazily. He realized, drunkenly, how he hated that house. "So long, Maw!" he screamed. "So long to you, Paw!"

He turned to Nance and Lizzy and bowed with a flourish. "Good night, ladies," he said, snickering and laughing. "Good night, ladieees, we're going to leave you now," he sang, and staggered down the trail toward Waynesville.

Nance just stood for a while, her arms folded, watching the fire. Lizzy's right breast hurt and she discovered a blistered patch on it the size of a silver dollar. Finally Nance spat some snuff juice on the dirt and turned from the burning house and started walking up the trail the opposite way from Dude.

Lizzy tried to pick up the clothes and the trunk and the

broken spinning wheel. "Where we going, Mama?" she asked, still crying.

"Got to find a place to stay," Nance said. "I reckon Jane will put us up."

It was cold and there was a white half-moon. As they walked up the trail Nance and Lizzy could hear snatches of Dude's crazy song.

"I'm leaving this trunk if you don't want it, Mama," Lizzy said. "Mama, you hear?"

Nance said nothing, so Lizzy put the chest down. "Maybe we can get it tomorrow," she said.

Suddenly Lizzy stopped and looked back. There were things still in the house, precious things she wasn't ready to give up. There was the baby doll Birch had given her fifteen years before, in the bedroom on the bureau Dude had made for her, and other things besides. But it was too late; the whole cabin was ablaze. The flames danced like a hundred mad demons into the dark sky.

It was an hour later when Nance and Lizzy came to the Putnam cabin, on the eastern edge of Jase Ledford's plantation. There was a lamp burning in the living room, and through the window Nance and Lizzy could see old Joe and Jane and their boy, Will, sitting around the fireplace. Nance just looked through the window and did nothing. Lizzy set the spinning wheel down and laid the clothes across it and went up to the door and knocked.

After a minute old Joe hobbled to the door and opened it and peered out into the darkness. "Lizzy?" he said. "Come on in. And Nance?" As his eyes adjusted he could see the clothes and the spinning wheel. He was puzzled but kept on saying, "Come in, come in."

Jane was sitting in a straight-backed chair by the fire. She looked up at Lizzy and Nance as they came in. She saw the burned places on Lizzy's dress. "What's happened?" she asked.

"House burnt up," Nance said, her arms folded, looking down at her worn-out shoes.

"Daddy left," Lizzy said.

The three Putnams looked at one another for a few awkward moments.

"I saved some clothes, and the spinning wheel," Lizzy said.

"Mighty cold night to be out," Joe said. "How'd it catch fire?"

"Dude done it," Nance said. "He was drunk."

"Was he mad about something?" Jane asked.

"Didn't have nothing to eat," Nance said.

"We had peaches," Lizzy said, and started crying. She felt such shame she wished she was dead. She wished Dude had got her with one of his bullets.

"Jane, we got anything left over from supper?" Joe asked.

"Done give it to the hogs," Will muttered, watching Lizzy.

"Ain't you got nowhere to spend the night?" Joe asked Nance.

"Nope," Nance said. She and Lizzy had moved over by the fire to warm themselves.

"Well, you're welcome to stay here," Joe said. "Mama don't mind, do you, Jane?"

"Nary bit," Jane said, but she didn't look happy.

"Maybe we can rustle you up some vittles," Joe said. His hand trembled as he poked at the fire with a green hickory limb.

"We ain't hungry," Nance said.

"You're welcome to stay here till you get straightened out," Jane said. "Maybe Dude will be back tomorrow."

Joe brought some quilts out of the bedroom and put two of them down flat in front of the fireplace and laid the rest in a pile between them. Then they all went to bed.

Will couldn't sleep for thinking of Lizzy, of her breasts and legs, of her uneven teeth and frightened smile. She was years older than Will. He had known her all his life. He often saw her in church and here and there on Jonathan's Creek. A thousand evenings he had taken the image of her to his lonely bed.

And now she was in the next room, in her scorched and faded dress, her black hair splayed before the fire. And she was down on her luck, at a disadvantage. The idea of it and what it could mean stirred him.

Late that first night he heard crying and he was sure it couldn't be Nance. He knew all about old Nance, as everyone did on Jonathan's Creek. He wanted to go to Lizzy and comfort her, kiss her, possess her.

He didn't sleep much that night and the next day he was sleepy-headed and irritable. In the evening he sat on the porch and watched Lizzy coming toward the house carrying water, one arm out, her flimsy dress clinging to her legs. The shape of her made him ache to get hold of her but he held himself back.

"You reckon Dude will come back?" he asked as she came past the porch.

"I doubt it," she said, setting the water bucket down.

"Where you reckon he'll go?"

"He's got some cousins on the other side of Waynesville," she said. She went around back with the water and poured it into the Putnams' big wooden washtub and started scrubbing. She had resolved to carry her load. Nance was in the kitchen helping Jane cook supper. She was carrying her load, too.

That night Joe stirred up the fire and Will brought in another log. Then they all went to bed, the Putnams in their beds and Nance and Lizzy on their quilts in the living room. Everybody went to sleep except Will. He lay still for an hour and then got up as quietly as he could and stood at the bedroom door in his faded red union suit and looked at Lizzy in the firelight. Her face was clean and pretty and her lips were parted just a bit and he could hear her breathing.

He stood there for half an hour just looking at her, watching the rise and fall of the quilt that covered her. He had never seen anything so beautiful. At last he went silently and knelt beside her, his heart pounding in his ears, his whole body flushed. He took her right hand and held it to his cheek.

She groaned and moved a little and then her eyes opened and looked at him. He froze like a cockroach but she closed her eyes again and he laid her hand back where it had been and went back to his bed.

Nance had awakened and seen all this; but she lay still.

The next morning, their third day there, Nance and Lizzy got up early and fixed a fine breakfast of eggs and biscuits and gravy, trying to do their share. When Joe and Jane got up and came into the kitchen Nance poured their coffee and filled their plates. Joe grinned and stretched and started eating. Jane sat looking a bit disoriented, but then she ate, too.

"It shore helps out, you all a-fixing breakfast," Joe said with his mouth full. "It's got to where it takes Jane all morning." He sopped his biscuit in the gravy and slurped at his coffee.

"Don't do that, Joe," Jane said. "It sounds bad, and we got company."

"Company? Hell, we've knowed Nance and Lizzy all their lives. Ain't we, Nance?"

"I reckon," Nance said.

When Will got out of bed and came into the kitchen Lizzy didn't look at him. He sat down and that left only one chair.

"Set down, Mama," Lizzy said. Nance went ahead and sat in the remaining chair and Lizzy took her plate to the window sill.

"Well, I'll have to say this," Joe said, and wiped the grease from his lips with his sleeve. "That Reverend Rabb is a fine preacher. He does a good job. Don't know where we'd get another one like him. He preaches God's word and don't back up a inch. Like Sunday—was you there, Nance?"

"No."

"Well, he preached on envy, which is shore a terrible thing. Like if I envied Jase Ledford, say, that would be a sin. And it'd be right foolish, seeing what that poor man's been through. And you know that Preacher Rabb has got a sense of humor about him, too. One time after a funeral— it was that Medford man's, the deputy's brother-in-law—I said to him, 'Well, Preacher, there goes another one,' I said, and he comes back, 'Hatch 'em, match 'em and dispatch 'em!' he says. Haw! 'Hatch 'em, match 'em and dispatch 'em!' I had a big laugh about that."

Will laughed a goofy laugh and Lizzy forced out a little chuckle. Old Jane picked at her food and had a sour look. Nance didn't laugh or smile, but then she never laughed or smiled anyway.

Nance and Lizzy fixed dinner and supper that day, too, and old Joe was very pleased. He chattered away about the war and told stories Jane and Will had heard a hundred times before. Though she liked being waited on Jane wasn't happy to have her job taken over by outsiders, however close she'd been to Nance over the past sixty years. But she intended to be civil.

Will was thinking of little else except Lizzy. He yearned to touch her, and yet he was afraid he might offend her and drive her and Nance away. So he was tormented.

That night he came again to Lizzy's side, and again he gently took her hand. She opened her eyes and saw his face above her, burning in the red light of the embers of the fire. He bent down slowly, watching her eyes, and kissed her mouth. She put her hands up against his chest to stop him but his kiss was gentle as a silent prayer and the insistence of his longing stirred her. After a moment of resistance she yielded to him. He fumbled with her gown, his hands trembling. Finally he entered her and he tried to hold himself back and tried not to cry out but it was no use. One second, two seconds, and he yelped, once, like a dog hit by a stick.

Then he held his breath and listened. Old Joe was rattling and snoring in his bed. Embers were sputtering in the fireplace. He looked at Lizzy and saw tears in her eyes. He felt ashamed and frightened. He pulled away and crept back to his bed, his eyes large with wonder. A mystery had lumbered past his dull mind—something huge and wild, like some beast that dwelt in the deep forest. He knew he could never grasp it. It was utterly too much for him.

Beside the fireplace Nance lay awake, too, her old face wrinkled and hard and expressionless. She had seen what happened to Lizzy. But she kept still and held her peace.

Chapter Eight

"I think I'll dye this one," Lizzy said to Nance. She was going through the clothes she had saved from the fire.

"What color?" Nance asked. She was sewing up the hem on one of Jane's worn-out dresses.

"Brown. I'm tired of this old faded blue."

"Walnut hulls and bark off of the tree," Nance said.

Old Jane was sleeping in bed, feeling poorly. The two men were out hunting squirrel.

"You like Will?" Lizzy asked her mother, out of the blue.

"You don't have to let him mess with you. We're doing our part," Nance said.

"I know that, Mama. But he's not bad looking. I mean, for a boy his age."

"He ain't but seventeen. Jane had him in her old age and he ain't got good sense. You don't have to let him mess with you just because we're in a bind. We can go somewheres else."

"Where?" Lizzy asked, putting down the dress. "Where can we go? What can we do? All your folks are over in Tennessee, and from what you've said they couldn't be much help anyway. So what can we do?"

Lizzy waited, hoping for an answer, but Nance went on with her sewing. She didn't have an answer.

They heard a horse trot to a stop outside. They waited and in a few moments there was a knock at the door. Lizzy went to answer it.

"Birch!" she said, and threw her arms around him.

He hugged her close and then looked down into her eyes. "I heard about the cabin," he said. "I'm awful sorry about it. I come by to see if, you know, there was anything I could do."

Nance went quietly out the back door and left them alone.

"What could you do now?" Lizzy asked. "We're settled in

here. We've . . . I've . . ." She turned away from him and folded her arms. She felt a sudden anger at Birch, who, she knew, was blameless. The truth she could not utter to him was that she had already given herself to Will Putnam. She couldn't say it and she knew that Birch was too innocent or simpleminded to understand.

"Come home with me, Lizzy," Birch said. "We could build us a house and . . ."

Lizzy burst into tears. She was burning with anger and shame. "It's too *late*, Birch. *Too late*! Why didn't you . . . How could you wait until *now*? It's *too late*!"

Birch didn't know what to do or say. He lowered his eyes. Lizzy went to him and buried her face in his chest.

The door opened and Will looked in at them. Behind him was old Joe. "Well, look here," Joe said. "Birch Phillips! Good to see you, boy! How's Zeb and Maggie?"

"They're fine," Birch said. Lizzy had turned him loose and was wiping her eyes. Will was glowering at them both, his neck and ears flushed red. He walked past them and put his gun in the bedroom, saying nothing.

"Stay for supper?" Joe asked, holding up two squirrels.

"Uh, well, no," Birch said. "I guess I'd best get on home. Old Jase Ledford's giving a party for Joellen. I got to run him off some liquor."

"Come back anytime," Joe said. Birch went past him and out the door.

That night Will didn't come to Lizzy's pallet, and the next day he was surly and mean-tempered. He stayed away a second night, too, but on the third night he came to her, as she knew he would, his passion for her raging. He held her down and quietly but forcibly took her, not caring how it was for her.

When he was through he lay heavily upon her and whispered, "Did you let him do that to you?"

"Who?"

"Birch Phillips."

"No."

"What was you crying about? Why'd you have ahold of him?"

"I was crying about all that's happened to me and Mama. Birch has always been . . . a good friend to me. Like a big brother."

"You and him was in here by yourself. Maybe you was doing it with him."

"We didn't do nothing," she said, crying again.

"Just remember who you're living off of," Will said. Then he got up and went to his cot in the bedroom and went to sleep.

The next day, toward evening, Jase Ledford rode up to the Putnam cabin. Joe was in his chair on the porch, staring open-mouthed out over the dead March countryside.

"Hello, Joe," Jase said, staying in his saddle.

"Howdy, Jase," Joe said. "How you doing?"

"Doing very well. What I come about, Lucille's throwing a little party for Joellen tomorrow night. Thought you all might want to come."

"I doubt if we can make it, Jase. The old lady's been

feeling poorly lately. She's in the bed now. Can't seem to come out of the kinks. But Nance and her girl might want to go, or Will. Oh, Nance!" Joe called.

Nance came out the front door with her arms folded and a twig in her mouth. Lizzy came out behind her, and then Will, all like sheepish children.

"Hello, Nance," Jase said. "I heard about what old Dude pulled. I hate it. Are you doing okay?"

"Doing all right, I reckon," she said.

"Hello, Will, Lizzy," Jase said.

"Hello, Mr. Ledford," Lizzy said.

"Reckon you all might want to come over to the house tomorrow night for a little party, for Joellen? I expect she'd like to see you all again."

"Don't guess we can make it," Nance said in her surly way.

"Guess there'll be a lot of folks there," Lizzy said.

"Maybe thirty or so," Jase said. "Some of Lucille's friends, some of mine."

"I might show up," Will said.

"That'd be fine," Jase said, and turned his horse around. "You're all welcome." He rode off, thinking about Nance, about how she still had some of that dark charm about her.

"A fine man," Joe said, leaning over his cane. "A fine man, that Jase Ledford. You ought to go to that party, Lizzy. You're a real pretty girl. You might find you a man."

"She's found her a man," Will said, leaning against the doorframe.

"She has?" Joe asked.

"She sure as hell has," Will said.

Something in the gray distance caught the old man's attention again and his mouth sagged open as he sank back into his chair.

The minister of the First Presbyterian Church, the Reverend Wilbur Jenkins, came to Joellen's party with his ugly wife, Daisy, and their two ugly boys. They were all dressed elegantly. And Zeb and Maggie Phillips were there, along with Birch, who was dressed up and very uncomfortable in a new suit. And John and Cora Hatley and their son, Aaron, and their two daughters, Margaret and Cindy, and the Janeses and their boy, Frank, and the Bramletts and their daughter, Laurie Jean. And Deputy Jack Carver and his wife and two small sons, and Lot and Ellen Ransom and their daughter, Lois. And there were the Longley sisters, Sarah and Janice, and others— friends and acquaintances of Jase and Lucille Ledford. Lucille didn't care much for Jase's friends, and he didn't care for hers, and the big dining room of the mansion seemed to divide up into the common on one side and the uppity on the other.

When Joellen saw Birch emerge from the crowd, pulling at his collar, she hurried over to him and kissed him on the cheek.

"You look so nice, Birch," she said.

"Glad to see you, Joellen," Birch said. "When you coming home for good?"

"In two years, when I graduate."

"I don't reckon you'll speak to a plain old boy like me then."

"Don't talk that way, Birch. You know I'd never change toward you."

Across the room, near the punch bowl, Lucille Ledford and Maggie Phillips smiled politely at each other as their husbands shook hands.

"Joellen has always liked Birch," Jase was saying. Maggie beamed.

"But she's met some nice young men in Atlanta," Lucille said in her bitchy way. "Oh, listen. It's Doc Crawford!"

An automobile chugged noisily up outside. Lucille opened the door and sure enough there was old Doc Crawford climbing down from his new 1910 Model-T Ford, the first automobile on Jonathan's Creek. Everyone piled out of the house to admire it.

"I reckon you've met some real smart fellers down in Atlanta," Birch said to Joellen after the excitement subsided.

She looked up at him with the same old look she'd always had. "Not really. Dora Macon's a girls' school. We're not allowed to see young men except at certain social functions, parties and such. You can't really get to know anyone that way. Not like I know you."

Birch looked admiringly at her. She was strikingly bright and pretty, and blond like himself. Her arms and legs were thin, fragile, elegant. She wore a party dress of light blue with a matching bow in her hair. She was clean and delicious-looking, like a fancy, expensive cupcake.

Birch couldn't help comparing her with poor Lizzy Hannah, with her black hair and muscular brown arms and strong, rough hands. Lizzy could never have been a college girl. She was a peasant, like him.

He was smart enough to realize that Joellen Ledford liked him, and he knew that his mother would like nothing better than to match them. And yet he loved Lizzy. He had always loved Lizzy. Then it dawned on him what Lizzy had meant when she said he was too late. She was lost to him now, gone to become a brood sow for Will Putnam. It broke his heart to think of it. He cursed himself for being so slow, for listening to his foolish old mother.

Maggie was jabbering away to Lucille: "Lucille, I'll have to give you credit for your broad-mindedness. You're a fine person, yes sir, I'd tell anybody that."

"You mean our missionary work? Well, I've always believed we lucky ones should share with the poor of the world, and should try to bring God's word to those in foreign lands. It's very important to me that . . ."

"No, I don't mean that. I mean you letting Nance Dude and her daughter live on your land."

"Nance Dude?"

"They call her that because she left Howard Kerley for that lowlife Dude Hannah. I guess she goes by Hannah now, but she never married him. Old Dude burnt them out and left and they moved in with them Putnams that live on the east end of your property. I feel like it's proof of how big-hearted you all are not to run her and her bastard daughter off. Especially since Jase and Nance . . ."

"Oh, bygones are bygones, I've always said. I never have been one to hold a grudge. Why, what does it hurt me for her to be living there? None, not a bit!"

"Well, I'll say it again, you're a big-hearted woman, Lucille Ledford, big-hearted."

While the two women were talking Jase answered the front door to find Will Putnam standing like a beggar, cap in hand, before him. Will was dressed in clean but worn overalls and a white shirt. His hair was wet. Lucille saw him a moment later, and her jaw clenched.

Will walked in and strode up to the punch bowl, and Joellen smiled politely and poured him a glassful. The punch by this time was nearly one-quarter moonshine.

"Howdy, Joellen," he said, grinning. "Your daddy asked me to come."

"So glad to see you, Will. How are you?" She put our her pale hand and Will shook it clumsily but sincerely.

"Doing real good. You learning a lot in that college?"

"Well, I'm trying to."

"You aim to be a teacher?"

"Yes."

"Miss Cordelia's getting old. You aim to take her place?"

"Oh, no, I'd never try to take her place, at least until she retires. Why, she's been the teacher here for forty years! She's just an institution here on Jonathan's Creek."

"You wouldn't want to come back in here, I guess, after seeing Atlanta."

"Oh, no, it's not that at all. I'd love to teach here, I really would. I just would never try to push Miss Cordelia out."

"You're mighty pretty, Joellen. You always have been, I mean, but now . . ."

The band started playing a Virginia reel and several couples paired off.

"Quick, Birch," Maggie said. "Go dance with Joellen."

He walked toward Joellen, but Will had already reached over and taken her hand, grinning, and she had little choice but to dance with him, leaving Birch standing in the middle of the floor looking foolish. He returned to his mother's side and observed the dark look on Lucille Ledford's face. Birch was slow to anger but he felt that he'd had just about enough of Will Putnam.

As for Joellen, though she found Will brash and rough-hewn, he was still a great improvement over the dandies and sissies she'd met in Atlanta. He had, for her, the kind of attraction that a snake has for a baby bird. She knew quite well that he was too far beneath her for anything serious, and yet she couldn't help delighting in her mother's obvious consternation.

And consternated Lucille certainly was. Clumsy Birch Phillips was bad enough, but Will Putnam was the last straw. She set her punch glass down with a clink, sloshing its contents on the tablecloth, and walked straight to her daughter and took her arm and pulled her away from Will and over to the wall.

"Look, little girl," she whispered, though all the guests were watching and listening now. "I don't care what you've learned in that fancy school. I will *not* have you embarrassing me in front of everybody. I will whip your tail for you, little girl."

Joellen darkened. "I don't know why you're so upset," she said. "How could I refuse to dance with him? Daddy invited him."

Lucille turned to Jase, her face flushed. "You just *must* ask that boy to leave," she said.

"No, ma'am," Jase said, rubbing his jaw. "I invited him. He ain't causing no trouble. You got your snooty Presbyterian friends and I'm putting up with them. The Putnams have lived here as long as I can remember. They're good people. If I ask anybody to leave it'll be that dumb-assed Presbyterian preacher."

Lucille turned in a huff and made for the kitchen.

Jase and Joellen exchanged a look. "Come here, Joellen," he said. She stepped up, her hands folded in front of her, and they eased away from the crowd.

"Your mama just wants what's best for you, Joellen," he said. "And I do, too. You're a young woman, you're almost grown, and you got a right to pick your own friends. It don't hurt nothing for you to dance with a boy. But Will Putnam, he's a poor boy. And a poor boy's always going to think you're something special, and, well, Will Putnam just ain't the right one for you. He'd never understand you. He's ignorant and he's a smart aleck, and a horse's ass. Somebody like, well, Birch Phillips, now, that's different."

"Mama thinks nobody's good enough for me," Joellen said, tears forming in her eyes.

"I think the same thing, Joellen. You got to make your own friends, your own decisions. But you've got good sense. Try to use it. Don't sell yourself short."

Jase put his arm around her shoulders and squeezed

her, and she smiled. She looked around the room. Will was gone.

Will walked home in the dark and sat on the porch in a chair and looked at the white moon and the dark clouds floating past it. The evening star hung brightly against the blue-black sky.

Will felt alive. Swirling in his head were the images of Lizzy in the darkness, Joellen in the light. Lizzy was the new moon, Joellen the full moon. His yearning for them churned within him; he wanted them both. He wanted to take Lizzy in the night silence and to walk and talk with Joellen in the light of day for all the world to see. Lizzy was his shame, Joellen his hope.

Too much had happened for him to grasp it all. All he could think or feel was that he was now truly alive, part of a vibrant, living world.

When all the guests were gone Lucille found Jase sitting before the fire, his boots off and his feet on an ottoman Dude Hannah had built for him.

"Jase Ledford," she said in her whiniest voice, "why didn't you tell me about Nance Dude living with the Putnams?"

"It don't hurt anything," Jase said. He had drunk a lot of Zeb's moonshine. "Dude burnt her and Lizzy out. She had nowhere to go."

"Does she mean something to you?"

"Naw. That old woman? Naw."

Outside, sitting in the front porch swing, Joellen was

luxuriating in the chill, sweet night air. She felt lovable, precious, beautiful as a fairy princess. She swung lazily and hummed "Beautiful Dreamer" and thought of Birch Phillips. Of course she loved him, she had for years—he was so sweet and kind, so strong and gentle.

But then something different stirred within her, a different feeling from love, and the thought of Will Putnam intruded into her pleasant reverie. He puzzled her and made her uncomfortable—his brooding face, his insolent grin and common manner, his body taut like a steel spring. He was different from Birch.

She forced her errant mind back to Birch Phillips, where she knew it belonged.

Chapter Nine

By the end of March 1910 Lizzy realized she was pregnant. When she was absolutely certain she went to Will as he sat smoking a cigarette after breakfast and put her arms around his neck. He looked at her suspiciously.

"We're gonna have to get married, Will," she said, smiling hopefully.

"Why is that?" he asked.

"I'm gonna have a baby," she said, watching his expression.

It darkened. He got up and walked out.

Lizzy was puzzled and hurt. She wept quietly as she washed the dishes. Nance knew what was wrong, but she said nothing.

Will avoided Lizzy after that, as much as he was able. He hardly ever spoke to her, and his manner changed to a kind of exasperated roughness that grew worse as she grew bigger.

In June Joellen came home for her summer break. Will was not so bold as to call on her, but he thought about her constantly, even—especially—when he made love to poor Lizzy. And he developed the habit of walking at dusk to the top of the hill that overlooked the Ledford mansion just to watch for a glimpse of her. He did this stealthily so that no one knew what was in his heart.

One day toward the end of summer, when Lizzy was seven months pregnant and Joellen was about to return to college, Will was watching the Ledford mansion from his spot on the hill when he saw Joellen walk to the stable and saddle up a horse and ride toward him. He hid behind an oak tree and watched her as she approached, her beautiful blond hair bouncing. She was giving the horse free rein and it seemed guided by benevolent stars right toward the tree behind which he stood.

In a few minutes she reached the crest of the hill and as she rounded the oak tree she saw him.

"Will!" she said, and laughed. "You scared me. What are you doing up here? Picking flowers for Lizzy?"

"Just come up to see what I could see," he said. His face looked like that of a naughty child.

"Like the bear that went over the mountain?"

"Ain't seen any bears," he said, missing the joke.

"I just had to get out of the house," she said. "The woods are so beautiful, so alive this time of year. I hate to leave them."

"They're pretty, all right," he said.

"Help me down?"

Will reached up and she slid down into his arms and he held her and kissed her, breathing in the sweet smell of expensive soap and cologne. She was so deliciously lovely, and her hair was so fluffy and clean, not like Lizzy's, which always seemed dull and greasy. The feeling of her thin arms and legs against him was a precious dream come true.

But she pulled away. "No, Will," she said. He pulled her back and kissed her again.

"You have a wife," she said. Her face was flushed.

"We ain't married," he said.

"She's going to have your baby."

"It ain't mine. It's somebody else's. It's you I want."

"It's impossible. I like you, Will, but . . . I want to be a teacher. It would be scandalous if I . . ."

She paused, searching for words, and he kissed her again. She kissed him back. Then she broke free and jumped on her horse and rode back to the mansion.

A week later Joellen went back to college. Two months

after that, on November 15, 1910, Lizzy gave birth to a daughter, Roberta Ann.

On that day Will went out hunting in the morning and when he got home at noon with his catch Nance was rocking the baby. Lizzy was in bed, exhausted and in pain, and old Joe and Jane were sitting in their chairs on the porch.

Will went past Nance into the kitchen and dropped a bloody possum on the table and then came back and looked at the baby.

"Boy or girl?" he asked.

"Girl," Nance said.

He sniffed and looked at the infant more closely. "Blond hair," he observed.

Nance said nothing.

"Who's gonna fix dinner?" he asked.

So little Roberta started life. As she grew she was sweet and cheerful and pretty. She seemed grateful to be alive. She loved music, and Lizzy and Nance sang to her every night at bedtime—softly, so as not to bother Will.

Will continued to be surly with Lizzy and Nance, and never had a kind word for Roberta. He always spoke of her as "that little bastard."

And he continued to moon over Joellen Ledford.

Joellen graduated from Miss Dora Macon's college in June 1912 and returned to Jonathan's Creek, not really knowing what she might do next but hoping Birch Phillips might somehow be worked into her future.

Lucille was convinced that Joellen had wasted her

time at college without finding a well-born young man. The truth was she had found several but simply didn't love them. She loved Birch, of course, and harbored dark and shameful feelings she could not admit to herself about Will Putnam. So she was in an unsettled emotional state. She could not understand why Birch was so slow and standoffish. But of course it would be absolutely unladylike for her to throw herself at him.

"If he never courts me, then I guess I'll just be an old maid," she said to her mother.

"Do you know how much we spent sending you to that fancy school?" Lucille asked. "Almost nine hundred dollars! And all you can do with it is become an old maid schoolteacher, like Cordelia Roberts."

Joellen laughed. But time went by. And though he loved his daughter Jase still drank and gambled. He didn't worry much about money, never had. Lucille worried about little else.

One day in July 1912 Lucille Ledford and old Suzy Jane stopped at Zeb Phillips's store for a bag of sugar. Lucille waited in the buggy while Suzy Jane, who was driving, went in. When she came back out with the sugar Maggie Phillips came out behind her.

"Howdy, Lucille," Maggie said, shading her eyes with her hand. Suzy Jane set the twenty-pound bag behind her seat and climbed back into the buggy.

"Hello, Maggie," Lucille said. She had always wished Maggie would call her Mrs. Ledford.

"Jase and Joellen doing okay?" Maggie asked. Lucille could tell she was working up to something.

"Fine, fine. How about your family?"

"Doing fine. Joellen decided what to do?"

"Well, no. I really think she should take a teaching job somewhere else, some nice town like Raleigh, or even Asheville. But, well, she loves it up here in these mountains."

"I love these mountains, too," Maggie said. "But tell me, how's that little Putnam family making out? I shouldn't say little, though. There's six of them now, counting the little girl, and old Nance, and Lizzy."

"Well, yes. I don't have anything to do with them. They stay there through Jase's kindheartedness."

"I understand, really I do. That thing between Jase and Nance—Lord, it was over with long ago. But what I aimed to tell you was this: You know last month that boy Will was in the store, and he had more than fifty animal hides to sell! Raccoons and squirrels and rabbits. He had thirty dollars' worth—at least that's how much Zeb paid him."

Lucille's eyes widened.

Maggie let the information soak in, then went on. "Now, you know we didn't feel quite right about it, because we knew he must have got all those animals on Jase's land, on *your* land. But Zeb said you probably gave your permission."

Lucille opened her mouth to speak but couldn't find words at first. "Uh, well, I'm sure Jase must let them hunt."

"It's a shame, them living off of you that way. You know what, Lucille? You ought to charge them rent. That boy Will, he could get him a job. He's young and strong. Now Joe and Jane, they're too old to work, of course. But it's a shame to see that boy Will laying around. He could get him a job down at the paper mill in Pigeon Forge. I don't hold with any able-bodied man not working at something. I figure if he's able to beget children, he's able to work."

The idea of rent appealed to Lucille. "Uh, how much do people get, for rent?"

"Well, the Brysons, that live on the Ransom property, they pay ten dollars a month. That's what I heard from Velma Bryson herself. And there ain't but four of them. You ought to get that much, at least." Maggie dearly loved imparting information and advice.

Lucille nodded and motioned for Suzy Jane to drive on.

At breakfast the next morning Lucille made her case: "Ten dollars would help a lot, Jase. You know very well, though I hate to remind you, you lose a hundred dollars a month at Dillard's Bar, and we still have to support Joellen, and there's Billy's family. And those Putnams are shooting our game and growing their garden and raising their chickens on our land."

Jase rubbed his eyes. Joellen ate her scrambled eggs quietly and ignored her mother.

"And besides that," Lucille went on, "if you don't do

The search party, April 1913. At right are Frank Janes and his dog.

Courtesy of Jack Best

The cave on Utah Mountain where Roberta Ann Putnam died.
Her remains are partially visible at lower left.

Courtesy of Jack Best

The Death Cell
Of
Roberta Putnam

Frank Janes outside the cave.

Courtesy of Jack Best

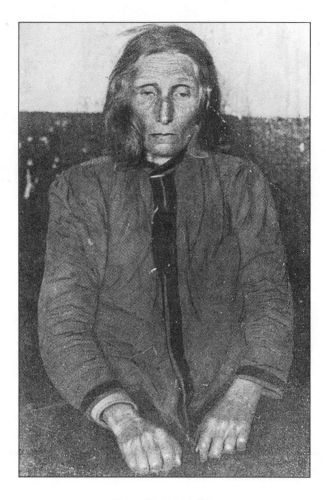

Nance Dude in jail in
Waynesville, North Carolina, in April 1913.

*Courtesy of North Carolina Collection,
UNC Library at Chapel Hill*

Nance at age ninety-two near her home on Conley's Creek,
pictured with one of her black dogs.

Courtesy of Naomi Franklin

NORTH CAROLINA STATE BOARD OF HEALTH
BUREAU OF VITAL STATISTICS

Birth No. 132 _____

CERTIFICATE OF DEATH

458

REGISTRATION DISTRICT NO. 87-00   REGISTRAR'S CERTIFICATE NO. _____

1. PLACE OF DEATH a. COUNTY Swain b. TOWNSHIP Charleston c. LENGTH OF STAY (in this place)	2. USUAL RESIDENCE (Where deceased lived. If institution: residence before admission) a. STATE N.C. b. COUNTY Swain
4. CITY OR TOWN Whittier Is Place of Death Within City Limits? YES ☐ NO ☑	c. CITY OR TOWN Whittier Is Place of Residence Within City Limits? YES ☐ NO ☑
a. FULL NAME OF (If not in hospital or institution, give street address or location) HOSPITAL OR INSTITUTION	d. STREET ADDRESS or R.F.D. NO.

3. NAME OF DECEASED a. (First) Nancy   b. (Middle) Ann   c. (Last) Kurley
6. DATE OF DEATH (Month) 9 (Day) 12 (Year) 52

5. SEX F   6. COLOR OR RACE W   7. MARRIED, NEVER MARRIED, WIDOWED, DIVORCED (Specify) widowed
8. DATE OF BIRTH 7-20-1848
9. AGE (In years last birthday) 104   IF UNDER 1 YEAR Months 1 Days   IF UNDER 24 HRS. Hours | Min. 28

10a. USUAL OCCUPATION (Give kind of work done during most of working life even if retired): Housewife   10b. KIND OF BUSINESS OR INDUSTRY
11. BIRTHPLACE (State or foreign country) N.C.
12. CITIZEN OF WHAT COUNTRY?

13. FATHER'S NAME Tom Connard
14. MOTHER'S MAIDEN NAME Elizabeth Tinney

15. WAS DECEASED EVER IN U.S. ARMED FORCES? (Yes, no, or unknown) (If yes, give war or dates of service) No
16. SOCIAL SECURITY NO.
17. INFORMANT'S NAME AND ADDRESS W.H. Kurley Whittier N.C.

18. CAUSE OF DEATH
Enter only one cause per Line for (a), (b), and (c)

MEDICAL CERTIFICATION   INTERVAL BETWEEN ONSET AND DEATH

I. DISEASE OR CONDITION DIRECTLY LEADING TO DEATH* (a) Probably Coronary Occlusion   few mm

*This does not mean the mode of dying, such as heart failure, asthenia, etc. It means the disease, injury, or complication which caused death.

ANTECEDENT CAUSES
Morbid conditions, if any, giving rise to the above cause (a) stating the underlying cause last.   DUE TO (b) _____   DUE TO (c) _____

II. OTHER SIGNIFICANT CONDITIONS
Conditions contributing to the death but not related to the disease or condition causing death.

19a. DATE OF OPERATION   19b. MAJOR FINDINGS OF OPERATION AND/OR AUTOPSY   20. AUTOPSY? YES ☐ NO ☑

21a. ACCIDENT SUICIDE HOMICIDE (Specify) none   21b. PLACE OF INJURY (e.g., in or about home, farm, factory, street, office bldg., etc.)   21c. (CITY, TOWN, OR TOWNSHIP)   (COUNTY)   (STATE)

21d. TIME OF INJURY (Month) (Day) (Year) (Hour) m.   WHILE AT WORK ☐ NOT WHILE AT WORK ☐   21e. HOW DID INJURY OCCUR?

22. I hereby certify that I attended the deceased from _____, 19___, to 7 June, 19 52, that I last saw the deceased alive on 7 June, 19 52, and that death occurred at _____ m., from the causes and on the date stated above.

23a. SIGNATURE Glenn B Hays   (Degree or title) M.D.   23b. ADDRESS Bryson City N.C.   23c. DATE SIGNED 9-13-52

24a. BURIAL, CREMATION, REMOVAL (Specify) Burial   24b. DATE 9-14-52   24c. NAME OF CEMETERY OR CREMATORY Bumgarner Cem   24d. LOCATION (City, town, or country) Wilmot   (State) N.C.

DATE REC'D BY LOCAL REG. 9-19-52   REGISTRAR'S SIGNATURE Mrs. Floyd Cunningham   25. FUNERAL DIRECTOR Moody Fun Home   ADDRESS Bryson City N.C.

Nance's death certificate. Note age at time of death.

something every bit of poor white trash in the county
will be . . ."

"Okay," Jase said, and finished his coffee, not looking
at Lucille. "I'll talk to them tomorrow. I'll ask them for
five dollars a month."

"That, or some of them have to leave. Especially that
awful old woman and that boy, Will. The best thing
would be if they all left. Then we could rent the house to
some sharecroppers and . . ."

"Okay. Okay. I'll talk to them tomorrow," Jase said,
and got up and left the house.

The next day he rode over to the Putnam cabin. Old
Joe was on the porch in his chair. Lizzy was sitting on
the steps with little Roberta in her arms. Nance was in
Jane's chair, her eyes closed.

"Howdy, Jase," Joe said as Jase dismounted. "Come up
and set down."

"I need to talk to you about something," Jase said. At
that point Will came out the front door, just waking up.
"What it is," Jase said, "is this: I'm going to have to ask
you all for some rent. Five dollars a month."

"Rent?" Joe said, his eyes wide.

"It used to be just the three of you. Now there's three
more. You're eating more. You're killing off a lot of
game. You're fine people and I wouldn't ask for it if I
didn't need it."

"We ain't got any money, Jase," Joe said. "There ain't
no way we can pay you no rent."

Jase rested one foot on the bottom porch step. "Will,

here, is a strong young man. He might see about working at the paper mill down in Pigeon Forge. Or he could help Billy out with some of the chores. Billy's getting old and could use the help. I'd pay him for that. It's either that or some of you will have to leave."

Everybody was silent.

"I know you all can understand. I didn't switch over to bright leaf like I should have, and Joellen's been in college, and I, well, I've had some unexpected losses." He couldn't help glancing at Nance, who looked away.

Jase got back onto his horse. "I'll come to get it the first of the month," he said, and rode off.

"What'll we do?" Joe asked the others after Jase had gone.

"It's easy to see who he wants out of here," Will said, looking at Nance.

"You could work, Will," Lizzy said. "Like Mr. Ledford said, you're young and strong."

"There's two here we don't need, as I see it," Will said. "The old woman and the baby. They eat but they don't work."

"I do my part," Nance said.

Will wiped his nose with the back of his hand. "I don't aim to go to work for no nigger. I'd be a nigger myself."

Tears came to Lizzy's eyes. "You're just awful, Will," she said.

"You better shut your mouth or you'll be leaving, too," he said.

"Now, now," old Joe said, "let's don't be short with each

other. 'A soft voice turneth away wrath,' that's what the Bible says."

"You don't know what it says," Will said to his father. "You can't read a lick." The old man clenched his toothless jaw and gazed off into the distance.

"I'll take the baby and go over to Tennessee," Nance said.

"Oh, no, Mama," Lizzy said, kneeling beside Nance's chair. "I can't lose you and little Roberta, too. I'll go with you."

"You got a place here," Nance said.

Lizzy put her face down on her arms and wept.

"We'll head out tomorrow," Nance said.

Chapter Ten

Nance started out for Tennessee with little Roberta on her back at sunrise the next morning, July 31, 1912. Roberta was not yet two years old. Lizzy stood crying silently at the back door. She didn't want to wake the Putnams—especially Will, who was ill as a hornet when he didn't get a full night's sleep.

Tennessee was eighteen miles over the south side of Cataloochee Mountain. There was a road that went from Waynesville through Jonathan's Creek right over Cataloochee into Hartford, Tennessee.

It was summer and the trees were fat with green leaves. Nance had three biscuits tied up in a rag and some clothes wrapped in a worn-out blanket. Roberta looked around with delight at the forest that closed around them as they started up the side of the mountain.

Nance calculated that she could get to the crest of the mountain by noon and then to Hartford by evening. She would try to find her mother's place before nightfall but if she couldn't they would sleep on the blanket on the ground.

Nance figured her mother would be eighty now, and her Aunt Mary would be even older. If they were still alive. They had never written, of course. They couldn't write, and Nance couldn't read.

And Elmer. He would be into his fifties. Nance had last seen him and their mother in 1876. Now it was 1912. She knew that was thirty-some years.

Elmer. Suddenly Nance thought she saw a movement in the darkness of the woods beside the road. She stopped momentarily and squinted at it. It was nothing. A drop of sweat rolled into her eye. She wiped it away. Then she went to a young birch tree near the road and pulled off a twig and stuck the end of it in her mouth and chewed on it as she walked along.

"Mamaw, Mamaw," Roberta said, and pointed at a pretty yellow butterfly. Nance ignored her.

She didn't like thinking about Elmer. She could see his awful, mangled face and the yellow teeth of the bear, and she could feel her mother's hands shaking her, and the words she said.

Nance shivered. She almost wanted to burst into tears. But she didn't, of course.

———————

By noon she and Roberta reached the southern crest of Cataloochee. The trees were thick and beside the road some ancient traveler had erected a small wooden cross. They stopped and rested and shared one of the cold biscuits.

As the sun was going down they reached the foot of the mountain on the Tennessee side. There was a rickety general store at a crossroads. Nance went up to the door, which was open, and went inside. A very fat man sat fanning himself. His fan had a picture of Jesus on it.

"Howdy, howdy, ma'am. That your youngun?"

"No. It's my grandbaby."

"Pretty little thing. What can we do for you? Want a cold drink? Got 'em over there in the icebox."

"No. I'm looking for Mary Finney's place."

"Old Mary Finney? Why, she died years ago. Years ago. Been dead ten years or more. Sorry. She a friend of yours?"

"My aunt. My mama was Kathleen Conard. You know about her?"

"She was the old woman that lived with Mary. Uh, she's dead, too; I hate to be the one to tell you. That means crazy Elmer is your brother. No offense."

"Is Elmer still alive?"

"Yes indeed, glad to say. He's probably out panning for gold, ha-ha!"

"Where does he live?"

"Same place the sisters lived. Go down toward Hartford to the second road on the right. Go a mile on that road and go across a little creek. You'll see Elmer panning for gold right there, ha-ha! Go on a half a mile and that's where he lives, where the sisters used to live. You aim to stay there?"

"I reckon."

The fat man wiped sweat off his brow with his pudgy hand and nodded. "It needs repair, that old house does. Cra—— uh, Elmer, he don't live like most folks, I better warn you."

It was twilight and there was the smell of grass burnt by the July sun and the sound of insects. By the time Nance and Roberta got to the bridge across the creek— Roberta was riding on Nance's back—it had started to sprinkle.

A hundred feet from the bridge was a man standing in the water toward the side of the creek. He would bend over and dig his tin pan into the sandy bottom and then hold it up and slowly pour its contents out, peering intently at his work.

"Elmer?" Nance shouted.

"Emer, Emer!" Roberta said, and kicked at Nance's back.

The man looked up at them, puzzled, and grinned and

waved. It was Elmer, his face even more horrible than Nance remembered. Now he was bald on the top of his head and had a scraggly beard and was skinny and filthy. His left eye was closed and sunken. His right leg was stiff and wasted away.

"Come here, Elmer," Nance ordered, and he splashed out of the water and hobbled to her and Roberta. He looked closely at Nance but no light dawned.

"I'm Nance. This here's little Roberta, my grandbaby."

"Nance? Haw! Nance!" He hopped up and down a couple of times. Then his face changed. "Nighttime. Got to go on home. Good-bye."

"We got to go with you, Elmer. We need a place to stay."

"You can stay at my house," he said. "Come on."

Nance was worn out, having carried Roberta the whole eighteen miles, but she plodded on behind Elmer. The road played out into a trail and then Nance lost track of Elmer. It was night now and weeds and bushes obscured the path. There was nothing she could do but push on through the brush in as straight a path as she could manage. In a few minutes she came upon a clearing and there was the house, completely dark.

"Come on, come on!" Elmer said from the open doorway.

"Ain't you got no lamps?"

"Got a lamp. Don't have no stuff to go in it."

Nance wiped her face and went into the house.

"Firsty, Mamaw," Roberta said.

"Where's your pump, Elmer?" Nance asked.

"Tore up. Get my water from the creek. Here's some."
He went into the kitchen and came back with a dipper
and Roberta drank from it.

"Goin' to bed now," Elmer said. "Been working today."
Nance saw him open a drawer and pull out something
and eat it. Then he disappeared into the dark bedroom.

It was her fault, Nance knew, and here she was where
she belonged, living with the consequences of what she
had done. Elmer was barely human. He didn't have
much more sense than a smart horse or dog. Nance always felt sad about Elmer but now she felt almost
beaten.

She took Roberta's hand and led her into the bedroom.
In the moonlight she could see Elmer's monstrous, idi-
otic form on one bed. The other bed was empty. There
was a mattress on it.

"Hungry, Mamaw," the little girl complained.

Nance heard vermin scatter when she set Roberta on
the mattress. "No! Animos, Mamaw!" Roberta said, and
scooted off the bed and onto the floor.

"Here, here. I'll put our blanket on it and everything
will be okay," Nance said.

It was chilly. Mountain nights are cool even in summer. Nance took her sweater off and put it over Roberta
and they both tried to sleep.

"Did you say your prayers?" Nance asked.

"No."

"You always got to say your prayers. You don't say 'em

out loud. God don't pay no attention if you say 'em out loud so other people can hear. What you say is, 'Lord, take care of Mama and Daddy and me, in Jesus' name, amen.'"

"Lord."

"Take care of Mama and Daddy," Nance said.

"Mama and Daddy. Mamaw, too?"

"Ain't no use to pray for me. I'll do that. Just you and your mama and daddy. Go ahead. Jesus' name."

"Jesus' name."

"Amen."

"Amen."

———

The next morning when Nance woke up she took the remaining biscuits out of her kerchief and ate one and gave the other to Roberta. Then she got a dipper of water from the big bucket on the kitchen table. In the daylight she could see how nasty the place was.

Nance went to work cleaning the house up and making a mental note of what was needed: coal oil, flour, sugar, on and on. In the pocket of her worn-out sweater she had twenty-eight cents.

When Elmer woke up he heard the sound of chopping. He went to the bedroom window and looked out and saw Nance swinging the old ax. He looked around and the place was cleaner than it had been since his mother died. He went to the cupboard and took out a nasty cracker and ate it and scratched his empty head.

Nance chopped an old tree up into fine kindling wood

while Roberta sat playing in the dirt. The child had developed a cough. Nance whacked away until she had hundreds of sticks a foot or two long and an inch thick.

"What you a-doing, Nance?" Elmer asked from the kitchen window.

"Chopping wood," Nance said. She put the ax down and sat on a stump and wiped her brow with the sleeve of her old polka-dot dress. Then she got up. "You got any string?" she asked.

"Nope," Elmer said, grinning. "You look old, Nance."

"I am old," she said. "Where's Mama and Aunt Mary buried?"

"Over there," Elmer said, and pointed into the woods. Nance went that way and looked around. Elmer came right behind her. "Right there," he said, and pointed to a clearing. There was a small cluster of white flowers and three feet away there was a stone, a round, smooth river rock. "Right there is Mama," he said, and sniffed.

"Where's Aunt Mary?" Nance asked.

"Same place," Elmer said.

Later that morning Nance got Roberta up on her back again, since she didn't trust Elmer to take care of her, and walked down to the store.

"You find Elmer?" the fat storekeeper asked her, chuckling.

"Yep," she said. "I need some string." She held out her twenty-eight cents.

"How much do you need?"

"About ten or twelve yards."

He measured her out a ten-yard length of strong twine and took all her money. Then he asked, "That little girl had any breakfast?"

"A biscuit. A cold biscuit."

"I give Elmer crackers. He ain't got sense enough to cook for hisself and I can't afford to support him, but I give him these hard crackers. I reckon he lives on them and water. It's a shame."

Nance left and walked back to Elmer's house and went to the backyard. She gathered the kindling wood she'd chopped into stacks of twenty or so. When she was done she had fifteen stacks. She tied them onto her back and took Roberta's hand and headed across the bridge and down the road toward Hartford.

Toward evening the storekeeper saw Nance coming up the road from town. She was minus the stacks of kindling wood, with Roberta on her back. He grinned at how she hopped along. Her face looked seventy but her little body was wiry and tough.

She bought the provisions she needed and back at Elmer's house she fixed the three of them a good meal. Elmer went back out to the creek to pan for gold until bedtime.

The next day Nance didn't do so well with her bundles of kindling wood, nor the next, and their meals were scant. There was no gun in the house and she couldn't hunt anyway, and Elmer didn't have enough sense to, of course.

But somehow they got by until winter, and even then Nance would take her bundles of kindling to town, and she and little Roberta would sit at their regular spot on a corner where lots of people passed. The well-dressed citizens of Hartford would see the miserable pair shivering and hear the child coughing and come up with ten cents for a bundle of kindling.

The first snowfall that winter was thick and deep. It stuck to the limbs of the trees and broke them down. Nance looked out that morning and knew she couldn't make it to town with Roberta so she sat in the house by the fire. Elmer went to the creek but it was too cold so he came home and sat with them.

Nance had bought provisions ahead when she could. She had enough flour for several days so she made them biscuits and gravy. Roberta picked at hers but Elmer ate like a hog.

Nance had three dollars in the pocket of her apron now.

Then one winter day Elmer said, "You all got to go now. This is my house." He gave no reason.

Nance waited and the next day he said it again: "You got to leave. This place is mine." He sounded angry, and he began to act surly and irritated with them.

Then the next day he took Nance's arm and led her to the door and pointed at the path across the bridge. "You got to go," he said.

"Won't be nobody to cook for you," Nance said. His grip was hurting her arm.

"Don't want you no more," he said. He went back and picked Roberta up roughly, and she cried. He set her outside the door.

"Why?" Nance asked, knowing such a hard question was futile.

"Because. This is my place."

It was a cold January day but Nance got her blanket and put Roberta into a sling on her back and started the return trip across Cataloochee. She didn't know what else to do but go home.

Halfway up the mountain snow started to fall and Roberta began coughing. By the time they reached the crest it was falling thick and fast and it stuck to Nance's shoes, which had holes in them, and piled up on little Roberta's head until Nance tied her kerchief around it.

Nance was tired and hopeless. It was a point in her life when she knew she had to do the right thing, it was up to her, there was nobody she could blame, nobody to carry her burden. She tried to think but all she could think of was getting home before dark. Otherwise the snow would finish her, and Roberta, too. So she kept walking. That was all she knew to do, to just keep on going, not stopping.

She didn't think about God. She knew the Old Man had forgotten her long ago. All the things she remembered from church seemed to be just pleasant stories. Not that she didn't believe them. She believed them, they were true, but they had nothing to do with the spot she was in. Praying did not occur to her, in spite of what she had told Roberta; she knew it was all just a matter of keeping on, keeping on, putting one foot in front of the other.

Two miles down the North Carolina side of the mountain the snow began to slacken. But the storm had slowed Nance down and she knew she would not make it to Jonathan's Creek before nightfall.

By dark she was very tired. She stumbled over a rock in the road and fell, and Roberta fell out of her sling and onto the ground and started crying softly. Nance picked herself up and stood a minute trying to rest.

"Hush, sweetheart," Nance said, and put Roberta back into the sling and hoisted her onto her back again. "Ain't no use to cry, baby. I know we're in a bind. Whining don't help none."

She started walking again. The snow was three inches deep and her feet had no feeling in them. Roberta kept coughing and wheezing.

Nance saw a faint light through the trees. She knew what it was and who it had to be. She trudged toward it for five minutes and then came to a small clearing.

"Birch?" she said. Birch Phillips scrambled and grabbed his shotgun and stood peering into the darkness. Nance walked into the light cast by the fire under the still.

"Nance? What in God's name are you doing out here?"

"Elmer run us off."

"Godamighty! Come and get by the fire. Put this blanket around you."

Roberta coughed.

"Is that little Roberta? Lord have mercy! You'll both

get sick and die out in this snowstorm. You're lucky I was out here."

Nance pulled the blanket around herself and Roberta and stood with her back to the fire. "I could use a swig," she said, and Birch handed her his jug. She took a big drink, and then another.

"You headed home? To the Putnam place?"

"Ain't got nowhere else to go."

"How could something like this happen, Nance? It ain't right, worth a damn."

"Jase wanted rent, lessen some of us got out. Will won't work, and he believes the child's not hisn."

"What? That's pure crazy. Lizzy's a fine girl. She'd never do nothing wrong. Whose does he think she is?"

"Yours."

"Mine?" He looked upward and the snow hit him in the eyes. "That's pure crazy. That Will must be plumb stupid. I guess I always figured that, though."

"He figures it happened that time he come home and seen you and her hugged up."

"Hugged up? Well, Nance, I'll tell you the truth. I asked her to come with me that day. But she allowed it was too late. 'Too late, too late,' she said."

"Will was already fooling with her then. She figured she had to let him because we was in such a fix, with noplace to go."

Birch sat quietly for several minutes. Then he said, "I'll get my horse and take you on home."

In less than an hour they rode up to the Putnam cabin. Nance got down with Roberta and stood a moment in hesitation.

"Let me know if I can help, Nance," Birch said.

Nance said nothing but went up to the door and knocked.

Jonathan's Creek Items
Cakewalk Scheduled

There will be a cakewalk at 7:00 on Saturday night at Jonathan's Creek School for the purpose of raising funds for much-needed schoolbooks and supplies. Hostess for the occasion will be the new schoolmistress, Miss Joellen Ledford.

Waynesville Clarion, January 30, 1913

Chapter Eleven

"**M**ama!" Lizzy said when she opened the door. "Oh! You must be froze to death!"

Joe and Jane were sitting in their chairs by the fire. Will was asleep in bed.

"Howdy, Nance," old Joe said. Jane said nothing. Nance and Roberta came in and stood by the fire. Roberta started coughing and it hurt Lizzy to see how pale she was.

"You been gone for six months, Mama," Lizzy said. She put her arms around Roberta and rubbed her little hands.

"Birch brought us a ways," Nance said.

Lizzy looked up. "Birch? He was outside?"

"Yep."

Lizzy stripped the child naked and patted her dry with an old rag and put some fresh clothes on her.

"How's Uncle Elmer?" she asked Nance.

"Ain't doing much good, to be frank," Nance said. "Ain't got no sense at all. He made us leave. We done all right while we was there, though." She looked at Lizzy's belly. "Looks like you're expecting again."

"Yes, Mama. Will can't say this one ain't his. I ain't been nowhere but to church since you left. Will's told me he'll marry me in June."

Nance looked at her and she said no more.

The following Saturday Lizzy was ironing a clean dress and Will was trying to put a shine on his worn-out old shoes. They were getting ready to go to the cakewalk at the school.

"I ain't marrying you till you get rid of it," Will said.

Lizzy hugged Roberta and put her hands over the child's ears and kissed her head. "She ain't a *it*. She's a little human being. She has a right to have a mommy and a daddy."

"Give her to Birch Phillips, then," Will said.

Lizzy knew it was no use to talk to him about Roberta. He was crazy, that was all there was to it. But he just had to marry her or else both the children would be bastards. Bastards like her. It would be better to send Roberta away than have her called a bastard. Life without a good name was not worth living, Lizzy was sure of that. It was better to be an orphan than a bastard. If she had to send Roberta away so Will would marry her, she would. And maybe he would grow up some, she thought. But Dude never had.

Nance was at the spinning wheel pedaling and spinning and trying not to think, but thoughts came to her anyway. What would Jase Ledford do when he found out she was back, for instance? He would want her out again but now there was nowhere for her to go. She couldn't go back to poor Howard Kerley.

Will went outside to wash his face in the cold spring water from the pump. Nance pedaled so hard that the pedal came loose and she had to get down on her hands and knees to fix it. Dude could always fix such things so easily.

Lizzy pulled her dress on over her head and smoothed it down. It was much too tight across her belly but it was the nicest one she had. She went to the kitchen window and looked out at their last three chickens, two laying hens and a tough old rooster, walking on the melting crust of snow, pecking hopelessly.

"You don't have to go," Lizzy said through the window to Will.

"Why, you might have that baby right there in the school, tonight, in front of everybody," Will said. "I'd hate to miss that. That'd shore be educational to them kids, now wouldn't it?"

"I know why you want to go," Lizzy said, pulling at her dress. "You figure you might get to dance with Joellen Ledford. Well, I don't care. Make a fool of yourself if you want to."

Lizzy looked at Nance, who went on with her spinning. "You going, Mama?" she asked.

"Nope," Nance said.

Will walked over to the Ledfords' stable and borrowed old Jonah, Jase's gentle plow horse, from Billy. Then he rode back and picked up Lizzy and they headed down the road toward the school.

"Will?" Lizzy said as they rode along, her big belly rubbing against his back.

"Yeah?"

"Do you love me, Will?"

"I reckon so."

"Let me keep little Roberta."

"If you want me to marry you you'll get rid of her."

"I hate being so poor, Will, and hungry all the time. Things would be so much better if you worked for Mr. Ledford."

He stopped the horse and turned to her. "I don't want to hear no more about that, or I'll just put you off and let you walk home. I don't see why you want to go to this cakewalk anyway. You can't dance in that shape. People will be laughing at you. Maybe you just want to see Birch Phillips."

She pushed her face against his back and tried to hold her tears.

"Don't get my clean shirt nasty," Will said. "Look, she'll be better off somewhere else. Maybe they'd take her over at the county home. And Nance, too."

Jonah got them to the school in half an hour. Jase had named the horse that because once when it was young it ate so much it almost foundered, and old Billy said it was like that man in the Bible that swallowed the whale. It was a fine, gentle horse.

It was dark on Jonathan's Creek when Will wrapped Jonah's reins around the hitching post in front of the school. Some menfolk were spitting and talking near Doc Crawford's Ford, and not far from them were young Aaron Hatley and Frank Janes and Frank's dog, Peedro. All of them had already taken a stiff drink of moonshine, except for Peedro.

The inside of the school was decorated with gaily colored paper and was very bright and cheerful, like Joellen Ledford herself. She was lovely and animated in the midst of a little crowd of local ladies and gentlemen, laughing sweetly and talking, utterly in her element. When Will saw her the old ache seized him again. He wished he were clean and well-dressed and educated and elegant. He yearned to touch her.

In the middle of the big schoolroom the desks had been shoved aside and there were fifteen straight-backed cane chairs in a circle for the cakewalk. Over next to the punch bowl were little Lois Ransom and Laurie Jean Bramlett. Laurie Jean was wearing a scandalous amount of makeup for a girl of sixteen.

Lizzy and Will picked a place near the wall and tried not to attract attention. They knew almost everyone but nobody came over to visit.

In a few minutes Aaron Hatley and Frank Janes came in the front door and made a beeline for Lois and Laurie Jean. The two girls remained aloof and sipped their punch. Lucille Ledford poured Aaron a cup of punch and turned away to greet some other guests.

"Golly," Aaron said to Lois, "this punch is so sour it would pucker a chicken's butt."

"Please don't talk like that, Aaron," Lois said. "It makes you sound so crude. Are you going to walk for my cake?"

"You baked a cake?"

"With some help from Mama. Are you?"

"I reckon," Aaron said.

In the corner a small string band started playing. Then in the door came Birch Phillips, with Zeb and Maggie. Lucille Ledford immediately rushed over to greet them.

Lizzy couldn't help watching Birch and as he looked around the room she caught his eye. But then Lucille grabbed his arm and led him over toward Joellen.

As Lizzy watched Birch, Will observed Joellen—her bright eyes, her smile, her clean blond hair, her pale, lovely skin. If she saw him she didn't acknowledge it with any sign.

"Pretty fiddle music," Aaron said to Lois.

"When they're played like that they're called violins," she said. "Do you waltz?"

"I reckon I can try," Aaron said.

Lois set her cup of punch on the table. When Aaron reached around her with his cup to do the same it slipped from his hand and onto the floor. He looked dumbly at the mess and then saw Laurie Jean and Frank pointing at him and giggling. His ears burned. He pulled out his pocket handkerchief.

"Leave it alone," Lois said. "They have someone to clean it up."

"I spilled it," Aaron said, "and I'll get it up." That about summed up his philosophy of life.

"Forget it and let's dance," Lois said. "The Ledfords' maid will get it."

Although he didn't feel right about leaving his mess Aaron went with Lois out onto the floor and danced. She smelled like lemons and rose water and he thought he might grow to like her almost as much as he'd liked Laurie Jean before Frank stole her.

When the song was over they returned to their place beside the punch bowl with Frank and Laurie Jean. Aaron noticed that the spilled punch hadn't been cleaned up yet. Laurie Jean was laughing.

"What's the joke?" Aaron asked suspiciously.

Laurie Jean grabbed Lois's arm and squeezed it, giggling and snorting. "Frank says Aaron dances like a pregnant cow."

"He does fine," Lois replied coolly. "I didn't see you dancing with Frank."

Laurie Jean composed herself. "Talk about a pregnant cow," she said, her hand over her mouth. "Look over there." She nodded in the direction of Lizzy Hannah. "She ain't no more married to that Will Putnam than I am."

Then the cakewalk started. "Listen up, friends and

neighbors!" Jase Ledford shouted. He held up a huge white cake. "This here cake was baked by Mrs. Maggie Phillips, and I'm sure it's a fine piece of work. Now come on and buy your tickets!"

When fifteen people had paid their nickels, Jase lined them up around the ring of chairs. The band started playing "She'll Be Coming Round the Mountain" and the participants walked around the chairs, laughing and talking and singing, until the song stopped, and then they all sat down.

Jase drew a number from a floppy Stetson hat. "Number four!" he hollered.

"Me! Me!" a frail old lady shrieked, and everybody laughed.

Will Putnam eased away from Lizzy and began to work his way around the periphery of the room, his eye on Joellen Ledford.

"This pretty cake was fixed by Miss Lois Ransom, Lot Ransom's little girl," Jase said. "So step up and buy your tickets!"

Aaron and Frank were among the people who paid their nickels. Jase signaled the band to continue, and the walkers went around for a few minutes until Jase waved the music to a stop.

"Twelve!" he shouted. Aaron's chair was number five, much to his chagrin. He had somehow expected to win, simply by virtue of how he felt about Lois.

"Me, hey! Twelve! That's me!" a nasal voice shouted.

Aaron was mortified to see Frank Janes rush to get the

cake. Lois went up to Jase's side and handed the cake to Frank and kissed him on the cheek. Aaron felt hatred blossom and grow within him. Frank was taller and older than Aaron, and more a man of the world, having been to Asheville lots of times selling produce at the Farmer's Market. He was always bragging about his great adventures and how much he was getting off the girls.

And what was worse was that he had already taken Laurie Jean away from Aaron. Aaron had given her up graciously. But now damned if Frank wasn't after Lois, too! It was too much. In his heart Aaron decided that it would be worth a few front teeth just to inflict some damage on Frank Janes.

The music began again. Joellen turned from the punch bowl and there before her was Will Putnam.

"Oh! Hello, Will," she said, smiling sociably. "It's good to see you. How's your family?"

"Okay, I reckon. Nice party."

"Thank you so much. I suppose you'll be walking for Lizzy's cake?"

"She didn't make one. Didn't have the fixin's."

"Oh."

"Right warm in here. And noisy. I aim to go out for some fresh air. Down by the creek."

"That . . . sounds nice," she said. He held her eyes a moment, then turned and slowly made his way toward the back door.

There was a loud crash. Aaron and Lois and everyone else looked toward the table and there was Lucille Ledford floundering around on the floor with the punch bowl upside down on her lap. Aaron knew that the old woman's rear end was soaking in the punch he'd spilled. He headed for the back door as Jase Ledford hurried to his wife's side.

Once outside Aaron stood in the dark with his back against the schoolhouse wall. There was a cool breeze and in spite of Lois's kissing Frank Janes he had to admit it was a fine night. He recalled the picture of Lucille Ledford's fat arms and legs flopping around on the schoolhouse floor and he couldn't help chuckling. He hoped she wasn't hurt. She was an old woman, after all. And besides it was his fault. He had spilled the damned punch in the first place, and then neglected to clean it up. He breathed in the cool mountain air and looked up through the trees around the school.

Then through the door beside him came Joellen Ledford. She slipped out quickly and eased the door shut behind her. Aaron stood still in the shadows, watching. Joellen hurried away from the schoolhouse down the little path that led to the creek.

Aaron couldn't understand why she should be stealing away to the creek. Through the trees he could see her blond hair in the moonlight.

Inside the school Jase Ledford helped his embarrassed wife into the supply room and calmed her down and sent Suzy Jane back to the mansion for another dress. ("The blue one with the white flowers," Lucille instructed Suzy Jane tearfully.) Then Jase left her there and returned to his role as master of ceremonies.

As the cakewalk proceeded Birch Phillips happened to notice that Lizzy Hannah was standing alone looking forlorn and pitiful. He didn't see Will around so he walked over and handed her a fresh cup of punch.

"Thank you, Birch," she said. There were tears shining in her eyes.

"Where's Will?" he asked.

"You should ask Joellen."

Birch looked around the room and back at Lizzy. He stared at her a moment. "Where are they?" he asked finally.

Lizzy looked down at her worn-out shoes. "I seen them both go out the back door," she said.

Birch turned and walked straight across the crowded room, past Jase and the cakewalkers to the back door. He paused beside Aaron, not seeing him, and lit a cigarette. Then he walked down the trail to the creek.

He found what he was looking for: Will had Joellen backed up against a maple tree and was kissing her long and slow, working his body against hers. The half-moon made a thousand little ribbons in the creek behind them, and it made a halo around Joellen's lovely, just-washed hair.

Birch paused to make sure he was seeing the situation as it really was. Then he stepped up and grabbed Will's arm and jerked him around and hit him in the face with his fist. Will pitched backwards into the creek and lay still.

"Oh?" Joellen said, her dreamy eyes clearing. "Birch?"

At that point Aaron stuck his head in the back door of the schoolhouse and hollered, *"Fight!"*

Will sputtered and scrambled to his feet and shook his head. Birch hit him again, bloodying his nose and knocking him back into the water.

"You got a wife, Will," Birch said. "And a little girl, and another baby on the way."

Will collected his wits and lowered his head and charged into Birch's stomach and knocked his wind out, and then got in a punch or two.

"Get him!" someone hollered. Aaron had brought the whole cakewalk assemblage to the scene. "Whip his ass, Birch!" another shouted. It was a fine occasion for the mountain folk, a real fight between two strong young men.

Joellen eased away from the fight. Among the faces in the crowd she saw her father's, pale with anger. She burst into tears and pushed her way through the mob and ran back to the schoolhouse.

Birch finally caught his breath and hit Will again, knocking him back toward the water. But this time Will pulled out his rusty pocketknife and opened it and went for Birch.

"I'll shove that knife up your ass, Will," Birch promised, panting. Both men were exhausted.

"You need to learn to mind your own business, Phillips," Will said, and slashed Birch's belly. Birch backed away holding himself, fear in his eyes, and then fell to his knees.

Aaron's father grabbed one of Will's arms and Lot Ransom grabbed the other and he dropped the knife. They dragged him toward the schoolhouse and left him outside and went back and helped Birch up and in through the back door. Maggie Phillips moved the empty punch bowl so they could lay her son on the table.

Lizzy went to Will and looked down at him. He was heaving for breath and working his jaw around with his hand. It felt gritty.

She left him and hurried to the schoolhouse. A lot of people were standing around Birch, including old Doc Crawford. They looked at Lizzy and there was a long silence. Her eyes went wide and she put her hands over her mouth.

Birch raised his head from the table. "It ain't too bad," he said. "It didn't go too deep."

Joellen Ledford was standing close. "I hate to have men fight over me," she said, and brushed a tear from her eye.

Lizzy backed out the door, wishing nobody had noticed her. She stood looking through her tears at the cold sparkle of the stars.

After a while Will said, "Let's go home."

Inside the school Doc Crawford wrapped a bandage around Birch's wound and pronounced him okay.

Chapter Twelve

"**W**ill's not such a bad person," Lizzy said as Nance fixed breakfast the next day. They were low on flour and there was no meat left in the smokehouse so she was stirring up cornmeal mush. "He's young, and he thinks he's supposed to do it with every girl he sees. And Joellen is so pretty and clean and all. I don't blame him too much."

"He ain't got good sense," Nance said.

Through the window she saw a dog. She put down her

bowl and ran out the back door but it was too late. The dog, a skinny yellow hound, had caught one of the laying hens by the neck and was dragging it away.

"Come here! Come back here!" Nance hollered. She ran as hard as she could but the dog ran faster. The chicken flapped and squawked, and the dog held it fast. After half a mile Nance fell on her face, gasping, and the dog carried the chicken straight on down the road.

An hour after breakfast that day Jase Ledford showed up at the Putnam cabin. It was a cold, miserable, drizzly day and a nasty gray-brown fog hung over Jonathan's Creek. In spite of the weather old Joe sat on the front porch with a quilt around him, and beside him sat Will in his shirt sleeves.

"Will," Jase said, not dismounting, "I'll be clear about this. You got to marry Lizzy or leave. She's the mother of your children, and you got to marry her or leave. And if you stay you've got to work and pay rent. And the rent's going up. It's going up to seven dollars a month. It's as simple as that. Where's Nance?"

Nance was sitting with Lizzy and Roberta before the fire but when she heard her name she came out on the porch. Lizzy came out behind her.

"Nance," Jase said, "you got to leave. Lucille says they might take you over at the county home."

Nance spat into her spit-can. In the house little Roberta coughed the raspy cough she'd had since she and Nance returned from Tennessee.

Jase turned his horse and rode home.

There was silence on the porch after he left. Then Will said to Lizzy, "I ain't marrying you till you get rid of that bastard child."

"It's not right!" Lizzy cried. "It's not Roberta's fault. And Mama does her part. She feeds the chickens and cooks and washes and cleans and everything. She works hard. She's always worked hard. You don't do nothing. *You're* the one that . . ."

Will slapped her and she staggered backwards through the doorway and fell. She picked herself up and went to the bedroom and threw herself on the bed. Roberta followed her, crying and coughing.

They had cornmeal mush again at their midday meal. Will grumbled some and when he finished with his mush he left the house with his rifle and went into the woods.

"It's not right, at all," Lizzy said to no one in particular. Roberta came up to her and put her arms around her legs.

Toward evening Will came back with a squirrel's tail sticking out of his pocket.

"Look, Roberta," Lizzy said. "Daddy's got us a squirrel!"

"Just one, that's all I could find," Will said, and took it and laid it on the kitchen table.

Nance set to work on it. She cut right up its belly and gutted it and then jerked its hide off and then cut it up and rolled the pieces in flour. She stoked the fireplace and put some lard in the skillet and set it on the rack over the fire and in a few minutes laid in the cut-up squirrel. While it cooked she poured some fritter cakes into another pan and warmed up the last of the canned beans they kept in a quart Mason jar. In half an hour she set the table and hollered, "Come on!"

Will came in first and sat at the head of the table, and then Jane, pale and sickly, and then old Joe, and then Lizzy and Roberta.

"Thank you, Lord, for what we are about to receive, and let us go in the strength of it to do Thy will, amen," Lizzy said.

"Amen," Joe said. Then he reached and got the two fat hind legs and gave one to Jane. Will grabbed the two front legs and gobbled them down along with a big helping of beans and two fritters. Lizzy got the back and broke it in half and gave one side to Nance and kept the other for herself. Then she pulled the smidgen of meat off the scrawny neck bone and put it into Roberta's hungry mouth. The child swallowed it and waited hopefully for more.

But the squirrel was gone.

Old Jane, glassy-eyed, started spitting her food back into her plate. The others turned their eyes away and while they weren't looking Roberta stole a fat bean from the old woman's plate and ate it, and then started coughing her pitiful, rasping little cough.

"Goddamnit," Will said to Lizzy. "Why don't you get her away from the table, coughing like that? It makes me sick." Then he belched. Lizzy looked at him with hatred in her eyes and pulled Roberta to her and held her and patted her hair.

"Damn!" Will said again. The child was sickly and dirty and there was snot hanging out her nose. Lizzy wiped Roberta's face with the end of her nasty little dress but it didn't help much.

"Some more," Roberta said, pointing at the beans on Jane's plate.

"That's all you need right now, sweetheart," Lizzy said.

Roberta looked around the table at each of the grownups, at hateful Will and stupid old Joe and sick old Jane, at her frightened mother and sullen Nance; and they all looked back at her.

"More milk," Roberta said.

"Got no more, sweetheart," Lizzy said.

Will got up from the table and went into the living room.

"Tomorrow I'll take Roberta to the county home," Nance said. Joe just looked at her open-mouthed, not comprehending. Jane's eyes were closed. Lizzy's were filled with tears.

Roberta was trying to steal another bean from Jane's plate. She looked up at Nance at the mention of her name. "Candy home?" she said, grinning.

Lizzy got up and went out the back door into the yard and kicked at a dried-up corncob. "I don't see why it has to be Roberta," she said to herself. But she could figure it out. Will was the man of the house, such as he was. Without Will they couldn't pay the rent and they'd all have to leave. And Jase wouldn't let Will stay without marrying her, because of Joellen, but Will wouldn't marry her until she sent Roberta away. And Lucille wanted Nance gone because Jase had once loved her. So Nance and Roberta had to go, it was simple, simple and heartless as a steel bear trap.

Nance came out, her arms folded and a stick in her mouth.

"Roberta don't eat much," Lizzy said. "And she's so sweet."

"Will says she ain't his," Nance reminded her.

"He's crazy, just crazy. I didn't do nothing with Birch. Just loving somebody ain't enough to get you pregnant, is it?"

"If they don't take her at the county home I'll give her to some nice family."

"Somebody with money," Lizzy said, pulling at her hair with both hands. "She's so pretty, surely somebody will . . . Oh, how can life be like this, Mama? How did we come to this?"

"I don't reckon I know. But it's got to be done. There ain't no other way that I know of."

"Old Joe and Jane stink," Lizzy said, sobbing. "They don't know where they're at. They'll be dead soon. Couldn't we just wait? Couldn't we just talk to Mr. Ledford?"

"Wouldn't do no good," Nance said.

"Will eats like a horse and don't do nothing. He eats everything up from the rest of us. Roberta's hungry all the time. And I am, too."

"She'll get fed good at the home," Nance said.

"It's like we ain't even human beings. I can't believe God meant it to be this way."

"Ain't no telling what God intended, but something's got to be done and I reckon it's left to me to do it."

Roberta came out in the yard and Lizzy picked her up and hugged her and rubbed her head. "You my sweetie, my darling?" she asked, and the child giggled and started coughing, and Lizzy held her close until the spell eased off.

That night at bedtime Lizzy and Nance sang to Roberta:

> *There was a lady, and a lady gay,*
> *Of children she had three.*
> *She sent them away*
> *To the north country*
> *To learn their gramary.*
>
> *They had not been there very long,*
> *Scarcely six months and a day,*
> *When Death, old Death,*
> *Came hasting along*
> *And stole those babes away.*
>
> *It was just about old Christmas time,*
> *The night being cold and clear.*
> *She looked and she saw*
> *Her three little babes*
> *Come running home to her.*
>
> *She set a table both long and wide*
> *And on it she put bread and wine.*
> *Come eat, come drink,*
> *My three little babes,*
> *Come eat, come drink of mine.*

> *We want none of your bread, Mother,*
> *Neither do we want your wine,*
> *For yonder stands*
> *Our Savior dear,*
> *And to Him we must resign.*
>
> *Green grass grows over our heads, Mother,*
> *Cold clay is under our feet.*
> *And every tear*
> *You shed for us,*
> *It wets our winding sheet.*

"That song don't make no sense to me," Will said. He was sitting on the floor with his back to the fire. "What's gramary? And who got the babes, Jesus or who? And where's the north country?"

"Gramary is magic spells," Nance said. "The north country's up in Scotland. It's Jesus that gets them."

"And what's a winding sheet?"

"What you wrap up a dead body in."

"That's stupid," Will said. "They don't wrap them up. They put them in regular clothes."

"Wibewood Frower," Roberta said, and clapped her pale, dirty little hands.

"Okay," Lizzy said, and she and Nance sang "Wildwood Flower" and then they all went off to bed.

Early next morning, Wednesday, February 26, 1913, Nance shook Roberta awake. It was very cold so she put four dresses on the child. She looked like a fat little doll baby.

Lizzy sat up in bed beside Will, who grunted once and sank back into oblivion. She rubbed her eyes and watched Nance putting the dresses on Roberta.

"Bring her here a minute, Mama," Lizzy said, and Nance led the child over to her mother. Joe and Jane were making rattling noises in their sleep.

"You be good, sweetheart," Lizzy said, hugging Roberta. "You'll be all right. You'll get to eat good and be warm and wear shoes. You have to leave because there ain't enough room and food here to go around. We're real poor people and can't take care of you no more. You understand?"

Roberta nodded and looked down at her bare feet and choked back a cough. Tears came to her sad blue eyes and she put a thumb in her mouth.

Lizzy held her close and started crying herself. "The county home is where you're going," she said, "or you might wind up in a nicer place even than that! And someday we'll be together again, I promise."

Nance took Roberta's hand and the two of them left quietly out the back door and started up the Indian trail toward Utah Mountain. Roberta trotted along in her four dresses like a little fat girl, trying to keep up with old Nance, who tromped along chewing on a twig, saying nothing. They passed the burnt-out house where Dude and Nance had lived and then went on up the trail past the Hatley place.

Cora Hatley, Aaron's mother, was in the backyard pumping water. She hollered, "Hey, Nance! Where you a-going so early in the morning?"

"Going over to the county home," Nance said.

"Got some kinfolks there?"

"Taking this child."

Mrs. Hatley quit pumping. "Come in and get warm," she said.

Nance and Roberta went into the house and sat at the kitchen table. Nance drank some coffee. Aaron and his two sisters, Margaret and Cindy, were still in bed.

"I don't believe they'll take her at the county home, Nance," Mrs. Hatley said. "I think they only take old folks."

Roberta looked up at Mrs. Hatley and then at Nance. Then she looked down at her bare feet.

"We got to do something with her," Nance said. "You want her?" Nance tried to smile at Mrs. Hatley, to make a good impression. Mrs. Hatley was floored. "Smile at Mrs. Hatley," Nance told Roberta. Roberta smiled at the woman, too.

Cora Hatley was asked to tell her part of the story of the murder many times, and she could never do it without crying.

"We can't take her, Nance," she said. "We got all the kids we can handle now."

Roberta had bags under her eyes and every few minutes she would cough a deep, raspy cough. She spotted two small wooden sticks over on the floor near the bedroom door. She got down from her chair and went over and picked them up.

"That's a whimmy diddle," Mrs. Hatley said. "You ever seen a whimmy diddle, sweetheart?"

"No," Roberta said.

"You rub this stick on the other one," Mrs. Hatley said, showing her. "You rub it this way and it turns one way, and you rub it this other way and it turns the other way. See?"

"Whimmy," Roberta said.

"Yes! Whimmy diddle. Aaron made that for Margaret. But you keep it. He can make her another one."

"We better be moving on," Nance said. "Much obliged for the coffee. Say thank you, Roberta."

"Fank you," the child said.

"You're welcome, sweetheart. Listen, Nance, I got some little dresses that Margaret's outgrown that she might could use. Just a minute." Mrs. Hatley went into the bedroom and opened an old trunk and got a few dresses and came out with them and she and Nance put them on Roberta, who held her arms up and did her best to cooperate. She looked like a pale little Eskimo girl.

"We appreciate it," Nance said, and she and the child walked out and down the trail that went over Utah Mountain.

Mrs. Hatley said later that she knew there was something wrong about Nance and the child, but she never had any notion of what Nance was about to do.

———

Nance and Roberta walked and walked until the child's feet were too sore for her to go on. She started to cry. Nance picked her up and put her on her hip and carried her that way. Roberta weighed about twenty-five pounds. Nance weighed about ninety.

Three miles up the side of the mountain Nance looked around and saw a man in a buggy coming up behind them. He wore a black suit and a brown felt hat. He had his horse's reins in one hand and a small buggy whip in the other, and on the seat beside him was a big, black, leather-bound Bible.

"Howdy," he said as he pulled up beside them. "You all need a ride? I can take you as far as my house."

"That'd be a big help," Nance said, and hoisted Roberta up and then climbed onto the seat beside her.

"Where you all a-going?" the man asked.

"Over to the county home," Nance said. "I got to take this child." She pulled her snuffbox out of her dress pocket and stuck a pinch under her tongue.

"Won't take a child, I don't believe," the man said. "Just old folks."

"See my whimmy?" Roberta asked.

"Why, that's a fine one," the man said, and smiled at the little girl.

"Reckon you could use a pretty little girl?" Nance asked, trying again to smile, snuff juice in the wrinkles of her mouth.

"Me? No, no, I don't reckon I could, no. Got two kids of my own."

They rode along quietly for a mile or so and then they came to a fork in the trail.

"I live down this way," the man said, and stopped the

buggy. Nance climbed out and then got Roberta down. "She appears to have plenty of dresses," he said. "But she needs some shoes on her feet, in this weather."

"Needing and having is two different things," Nance said, and spat. The man popped his little whip and the horse ambled down the smaller trail toward a cabin.

Nance put Roberta up on her back and made her way over the ridge of Utah and down the other side about half a mile and then sat down, exhausted. After she'd rested a few minutes she took Roberta's hand and led her off the trail and out onto a little hump that stuck out of the mountain, where the granite showed through the bare trees of winter. It looked just as it had almost fifty years before, that spring of the year she'd married poor Howard Kerley, except that now there were no pretty wildflowers. The little cave was still there.

Roberta looked into the dark hole in the rocks. Nance scooped up an armful of damp leaves and put them into the cave. "Come here, honey," she said.

"Me don't like," Roberta said.

"Come on," Nance said, and grabbed her arm and pulled her toward the cave.

"Don't like! Want candy home!"

"Come on. I got to leave you here so I can go over to the county home and see if they'll take you. I can't carry you the whole way. I'm wore out."

Roberta hesitated.

"Come here. That's right. Go on now, right back in there, as far as you can get."

Roberta went on into the cave, whining a little and starting to cry.

"I got to put some rocks over the hole so a bear won't get you," Nance said. Roberta squatted at the back of the cave, crying. She still had the whimmy diddle.

Nance saw some big rocks a few feet down the side of the cliff so she scooted down and rolled them up, one at a time, and pretty soon the mouth of the cave was covered. She was bone-tired when she was done so she sat and rested awhile. She broke a twig off a dead limb and put it into her mouth. She could hear Roberta crying softly in the cave.

"Mamaw?" the child's tiny voice said, but Nance didn't answer. "Don't leave baby, Mamaw. Please?"

"Be quiet, Roberta, or that old bear will hear you and come and get you and eat you up."

Roberta sobbed and coughed and begged. "Sorry, Mamaw, sorry. Don't leave baby. Please, please."

"There's a lot you won't have to go through," Nance said, but not loud enough for the child to hear. Then she climbed her way back to the trail and went over the ridge of the mountain and back toward Jonathan's Creek.

Around noon that day Nance got back to the Putnam cabin. Lizzy was sitting on the porch, knitting a sweater. "Did they take her?" she asked, standing up.

"Yep," Nance said. "They took her."

"You're back awful quick," Lizzy said.

"Feller give us a ride."

"Who was it?"

"Feller in a buggy that lives up the side of the mountain. Didn't know him."

"That was nice of him."

"Yep. A fine feller," Nance said, sitting in Jane's chair. Lizzy sat, too.

"He rode you all the way? To the county home?"

"Yep."

"And back?"

"Yep."

"I started Roberta this sweater. Maybe we'll go see her so I can give it to her."

"Best to leave her be, the man said."

"Who said?" Lizzy asked.

"The man that runs the county home," Nance said. She still had a twig between her teeth.

"Oh," Lizzy said.

On the other side of Utah Mountain, on the side of the protuberance known as Ad Tate Knob, Roberta sat in the dark. She was being good and quiet except for coughing now and then. She didn't want the bear to get her. She didn't know what a bear looked like but she knew it was something bad. She shivered in the February cold and worked her thin little body around in her seven dresses.

She felt around among the leaves and found the whimmy diddle and held the two sticks and rubbed them together but it was too dark to see. Finally she laid the toy aside and snuggled down in the damp, cold leaves and dozed off.

Chapter Thirteen

Dude was buried beside his mother and father next to
the burnt-out house on Jonathan's Creek.

The *Clarion* didn't mention Nance, nor did it mention
Dude's cousins, who paid for the funeral. Frady's Funeral Home had supplied the obituary information. Henry
Frady knew that Dude had a daughter who lived on the
Ledford farm, so he called Lucille, his niece; and Lucille,
to save appearances, told him poor Lizzy was married to
the Putnam boy, which of course was premature. When
Lizzy read the notice she was delighted to see herself
mentioned as a Putnam and decided it was high time she

took the name, considering she was pregnant by Will for the second time.

Lizzy wanted to go to the burial but she was just too big. She sat that day in the kitchen, doing nothing. She remembered some good times, times when Dude had come home sober. But most of the time he had come home angry and drunk.

When it got dark that first night in the rock cleft Roberta began to cry. She was afraid to try to scratch her way out because of the bear Nance had told her about. She could tell it was night because the sunlight no longer shone through the cracks between the big rocks.

"Mamaw?" she said quietly. Then, "Mama?" She waited; then she screamed out, *"Maamaaa!"*

Lizzy sat upright in bed beside Will, her eyes wide. She couldn't immediately tell where she was because of the total darkness of the room. It was almost like a grave. But then she saw the moon through the bedroom window and realized who and where she was and why she was there. Then she was seized with fear for Roberta and started trembling.

Across the bedroom on her cot was Nance, a silver moonbeam on her wrinkled face. Old Joe and Jane were rattling and wheezing in their sleep.

It hit Lizzy suddenly what it was that was wrong. It was fifteen miles across Utah Mountain to the county home. Even a horse going five miles an hour—which a horse couldn't do up the side of Utah—would take three hours there and three hours back, a total of six hours. And Nance was back in five.

She hugged herself and snuggled down under the covers. What had Nance done with Roberta? Lizzy tried to tell herself she was wrong. She thought about Miss Cordelia Roberts, her old teacher, about how Miss Cordelia would approach arithmetic with her clean, pure logic. Lizzy wished she had her slate. She went through the calculation again in her head and it added up to one thing: Nance had not taken Roberta to the county home.

She thought of Roberta's blond hair and blue eyes. They were like Birch's. She wondered suddenly about that time he'd come to visit, when she held him. Could she have conceived Roberta in that small, precious moment? His hands, his strong, slow arms, oh God, could it have happened then? Could such a thing happen?

Will snorted and shifted in the bed beside her. He was childish and selfish but he was only a boy. Birch was a man. Will would marry her now, Lizzy thought; but now it didn't seem to matter.

She realized that she wanted Roberta with her. The county home would surely give her back. But Roberta was not at the county home, and Lizzy knew it.

On the morning of February 27 Roberta woke up and found she was still in the bad place. It was daylight. She was hungry and she thought about biscuits and gravy and her stomach started growling.

Mamaw had not come back for her.

She crawled the two or three feet to the front of the cave, where the rocks were piled up, and felt around and pushed at them. Some small rocks and pieces of dirt fell away and so she pushed harder but the big rocks wouldn't budge.

"Mamaw?" she shouted, tears coming to her eyes. "Mama? Daddy?"

Then she listened.

Nothing.

Those were all the real people she knew. It was no use hollering for old Joe or Jane. They never heard anything anyway.

Then she wailed with all her might, *"Maaamaaaa!"*

A month later people in the valley below would claim they heard what sounded like a child crying both night and day on that Thursday, February 27, 1913. And they would tell about it for years. For generations.

The next morning Will decided to go over the hill to help old Billy milk Jase Ledford's cows. Lizzy would normally have viewed that as a positive sign, but she was too worried about Roberta.

When Will got back from his milking Nance was fixing breakfast, trying to make one egg and some flour and grease and water go as far as it could. Lizzy was knitting. Will washed his hands at the pump and came into the house through the back door.

"Still knitting that little bastard a sweater?" he asked. "She's gone. You need to be knitting me one."

Lizzy bit her lip and kept her peace. Will sat down before the fireplace and put his feet up on the bricks.

"How you feeling, Maw?" Will asked his mother, who was nodding beside Joe. She didn't answer. Will stood up and got a quilt and put it around her shoulders. Her eyelids flickered and her mouth smacked but she was not aware of her son. In her darkened mind she was riding in a wagon and all around her were Union soldiers, their faces pale and stern.

"When's breakfast going to be ready?" Will hollered at Nance.

"Soon," Nance answered from the kitchen.

"Wouldn't they take you at the home?" he hollered.

"Nope," Nance said.

"Too damn ugly," Will muttered, and grinned to himself.

"I seen Robert E. Lee," old Joe burst out. "And Joe Johnston. I never seen Sherman, though."

Will jumped up and slapped the knitting needles from Lizzy's hands. He looked around wildly and then he picked up the needles and yarn and opened the front door and threw them out into the dirt. "Now forget her! She's gone."

Jane started coughing. She coughed and coughed.

"Come on to breakfast!" Nance hollered from the kitchen.

In the cave Roberta started scratching in the dirt in the places where the light came through. Her fingers bled and she sucked the blood from them. She coughed and hurt all over and she needed to go to the toilet.

She crawled to the back corner of the cave and went, and when she was through she was proud of herself and knew her mommy would say she was a good girl because she had remembered not to go in her clothes. But after a while she realized that she must have done something bad, so bad that Mommy didn't care anymore whether she went on herself. But she didn't know what she had done.

"Sorry," she said, and listened. A cold breeze whistled through the spaces between the rocks. "Baby sorry," she said.

The Putnam cabin was quiet that night. Not long after sundown Will and Joe and Jane went off to bed, leaving Nance and Lizzy sitting before the dying fire. Nance rocked slowly and said nothing. She seemed even quieter than usual, if that was possible. It was the time of night when Lizzy would sing softly to little Roberta.

"Where'd you learn them old songs, Mama?" Lizzy asked. "Like 'Lady Gay' and 'Barbara Allen' and such?"

"My mama sung them to me," Nance said. "She allowed as how she figured they was from Scotland."

"Some of them are real pretty and sad."

"Yep," Nance said.

They sat quietly for a few minutes and then Lizzy

went to the front door and went out into the yard and looked around in the dark for her knitting.

Up on Utah Mountain that night Roberta was holding her breath and listening. Something was sniffing and scratching at the rocks. There was a space in between through which she could see the stars, but something had come and blotted them out and there was only darkness and the sniffing.

It was after her. It was not a person. It sniffed and scratched at the rocks of her small dungeon.

Three weeks passed. It was Palm Sunday. In the early afternoon the members of the Baptist church met on the bank of Jonathan's Creek for a baptismal service. Nance and Lizzy were there, and Birch and Zeb and Maggie, and the Hatley family, and the Bramletts, and Lois Ransom and her family, and Frank Janes and his dog, Peedro, and some other folks.

The first to be baptized was Laurie Jean Bramlett. As she walked down into the cold water of the creek her dress floated up and Aaron Hatley saw her white drawers. He tried not to look, having just recently accepted the Lord. He couldn't help thinking about it, though, and he felt very guilty and unworthy. A saved person, he felt, steered his mind clear of sins of the flesh. He looked over at sweet little Lois Ransom. He really loved Lois. His feelings for Laurie Jean had been mostly physical.

Laurie Jean was a dull girl and Aaron's thoughts of her had always been shameful and lustful.

Preacher Rabb held a white handkerchief over Laurie Jean's nose and mouth and let her down backwards, gently, into the creek. Aaron could see chill bumps on her arms. The preacher said, "I baptize thee, Laurie Jean, in the name of the Father, and of the Son, and of the Holy Ghost." And then he pulled her back upright. Her dress was all wet and her breasts stood out full and firm.

As he waded out to join the preacher Aaron knew in his heart that he was not right with the Lord, and he tried to pray for forgiveness. The preacher held out his hand and Aaron took it. He looked back at the congregation on the bank and watched Laurie Jean step onto the bank. Her father had a quilt and put it around her.

The preacher was shaking with the cold as badly as Aaron was. He put a dry handkerchief over Aaron's face and let him down, but Aaron's foot slipped on a slick rock and the preacher dropped him and he fell backwards into the icy water. Aaron couldn't swim and he panicked and breathed in water and splashed and struggled and gasped like a person possessed by a demon.

The people on the bank all laughed, especially Frank Janes, who was now standing beside Lois.

Aaron couldn't breathe. The preacher grabbed him by his shirt and dunked him again and held him under long enough to say, "I baptize thee, Aaron," and so on. Then he brought him back up.

"Just relax," Preacher Rabb said. "You're okay."
Aaron coughed and spat as the preacher led him out of
the water. Everybody was laughing.

"Let us sing 'Rock of Ages,'" the preacher said, still
shaking.

Everybody sang,

> *Rock of Ages, cleft for me,*
> *Let me hide myself in Thee.*
> *Let the water and the blood,*
> *From Thy riven side which flowed,*
> *Be of sin the double cure,*
> *Save from wrath and make me pure.*
>
> *While I draw this fleeting breath,*
> *When mine eyes shall close in death,*
> *When I rise to worlds unknown,*
> *And behold Thee on Thy throne,*
> *Rock of Ages, cleft for me,*
> *Let me hide myself in Thee.*

Then the preacher launched into a little sermon and
then a prayer. While all heads were bowed Lizzy made
her way to Birch's side.

"Birch," she said, "please take this to Roberta at the
county home." She handed Birch the sweater she had
finished in secret.

"Sure," Birch said, and put it into his shirt.

"And see if she's all right."

"Okay."

Then the prayer was over and the people walked up the hill toward the church.

"If you'd a-got drownded, at least you'd a-gone to heaven," Zeb Phillips said to Aaron, and everybody laughed some more.

Aaron walked along in shame beside his two sisters to the family wagon. He looked sheepishly for Lois and saw her and when she grinned and waved he felt much better. He had concluded that nobody who saw his baptism would ever speak to him again.

He asked himself if he still hated Frank Janes for taking Laurie Jean away from him and was surprised to find that his ill will was not as strong as before. A flower of joy had blossomed in his heart.

Up ahead walked Lizzy and Nance, not speaking. Lizzy was very big now and Nance looked like an Indian squaw with her solemn look and her arms folded over her breasts.

"What's that Lizzy Putnam give you?" Maggie asked Birch on the way home.

"A sweater," he said. "She wants me to take it to the county home, to the little girl."

"You know what I think? I don't think she took that youngun to the county home," Maggie said.

Zeb was driving the wagon. "Now, Mother, that's not Christian, to suspect people like that," he said. "Where else would the little girl be?"

"We'll find out. We'll see who's Christian and who

ain't. You know what Cora Hatley told me on the telephone yesterday? Old Nance stopped by her house with
the child that morning. She said Nance tried to give her
the little girl. And then she come back at noon. Alone.
Nance wasn't gone long enough to get to the county
home and back. Cora says Nance done something else
with that baby."

"That's all guesswork," Zeb said.

"We'll see. And who was Lizzy hiding that sweater
from? What's the big secret about a sweater?"

"There's a letter in it," Birch said, and regretted it
immediately.

"Let's see it."

"It ain't to you, Mother," Zeb said. "It ain't none of
your business."

"Give it here," she ordered Birch, and he handed it over.
Maggie read it aloud:

> Dear Friends,
>
> I want to thank you all for taking in my little
> Roberta. We are having a right hard time over
> here on Jonathan's Creek which I guess my moth-
> er told you about and looked like there was noth-
> ing else we could do but give her up.
>
> Mr. Jase Ledford who owns our place claimed
> there was too many of us living here and was
> fixing to raise our rent, and there was other stuff
> too which I will not burden you with our troubles.
>
> I know you will take good care of her. She likes

to be sung to at night and I fully expect that cough to wear off. This sweater I am sending is for her. I don't plan coming to bother you all or nothing for I know it is best not to look back.

But please tell Roberta her Mother loves her just like always. I know you all will love her and be good to her. In Christian love,

Lizzy Putnam

Three days later Birch got around to taking the sweater to the county home. He rode over on a plow horse and it took him three hours to get there.

The county home was a big, square brick building with a flower garden in front. None of the flowers were blooming yet. There were three old men and five old women in the yard and on the porch, moving about slowly or sitting and rocking, or just sitting. Birch went in the front door and a stout, busy little woman of fifty or so greeted him.

"I've come to bring this to little Roberta Putnam," he said. "She ain't mine, I come for her mother, Lizzy."

"We don't have no such person here," the little woman said cheerily. "We don't have nothing but real old folks and sick people."

"She ain't here? You don't have no little blond-haired girl, about two or three years old?"

"No sir, I'm sorry." The woman seemed sincerely distressed not to be able to help him.

Birch stood there a minute, looking around him. There were two old women in nightgowns, and an old man was peeing on the floor beside them.

"Is there a child lost?" the little lady asked, smiling.

"Looks like it," Birch said, and left.

When he got home he stopped on the porch and told his mother what had happened.

"Not there?" Maggie said. "I told you. You could have called them up and saved yourself a trip. I told you it wouldn't be there. That old woman has done something bad with that child. It's been gone since February twenty-sixth, which was a Monday. Now it's March twenty-first. That's almost a month. You know, I heard something that night, the night Nance took that baby off. I heard crying."

"Now, now, Mother," Zeb said. "Calm down. There's a simple explanation. You're jumping to conclusions."

"I ain't doing no such thing. Something's rotten in Jonathan's Creek. Even Lizzy don't know where her own child is at. I think Lucille Ledford ought to know about this." She got up and went inside to the telephone.

"No!" Zeb hollered. "This ain't none of your business! You just stay off of that telephone, or I'll jerk the damn thing off of the wall!"

Maggie stopped and, disgruntled, went back out onto the porch and sat down.

"Telephones are the work of the devil, I'm convinced of

it," Zeb said. "Used to be if women wanted to gossip they'd at least have to walk a ways. Now they can work their jaws without leaving home. I don't think we ought to keep it, no sir, I don't."

Birch got up and went to his horse and rode up the Indian trail toward the Putnam cabin. There was plainly somebody Lizzy didn't want to know about the sweater, and he didn't know how he could return it and tell her what he had found out and still keep the whole business a secret. He figured he had better tell Lizzy what he knew and let the rough end drag.

Why would a mother send her own daughter away? It just didn't fit his image of Lizzy.

When Zeb finally nodded off to sleep in his rocking chair Maggie sneaked into the house and went to the telephone, which was on the kitchen wall, and turned the crank twice.

"I need to talk to Lucille Ledford," she said when the operator answered.

When Birch got to the Putnam cabin he hesitated at the edge of the woods for a moment. He could see Lizzy and Jane rocking on the porch. Then he saw Will walking over the hill toward the Ledford mansion. He goosed his horse and rode up to the cabin.

Old Jane didn't even look up from whatever thoughts occupied her. Lizzy stood up and was about to run down the steps but stopped and crept down slowly.

"What'd they say?" she asked in a whisper.

"She ain't there," Birch said.

Lizzy put her hands over her eyes. "I knew she wasn't there," she said. "I knew it."

Birch got down from his horse and put his hand on Lizzy's shoulder. He didn't know what to say.

"*Mama!*" Lizzy screamed out. "*What'd you do with Roberta? What'd you do? Mama!*"

Nance came out on the porch. She had been working at the spinning wheel.

"Mama," Lizzy said, crying, "what did you do with my Roberta? She's not at the county home. Where *is* she?"

Nance folded her arms over her breasts and chewed on the stick in her mouth and glared at Birch. Birch scratched his chin and looked back at her.

"Please, Mama, what'd you do with her?"

"I give her to a man in a buggy," Nance said.

Lizzy and Birch just looked at her.

"The man that gave you the ride?" Lizzy asked.

"Yep," Nance said. "He allowed as how he wanted a little girl. So I give her to him."

"What was his name?" Lizzy asked.

"I ain't got no idea. It didn't make no difference to me. He's gone from here anyway."

"What did he look like?" Birch asked.

"He was dressed all in black. Tall and skinny. Had a big Bible on the seat beside of him."

"Sounds like that Holiness preacher, Fincher," Birch

said. "He lives about halfway up the side of Utah. He's just been here a few months. I've seen him in Waynesville. Seemed like a pretty nice feller."

Lizzy was wiping her eyes. "Will you go up there with me, Birch?" she asked.

He looked at her for a long moment, and then at Nance.

"I don't believe that it was him," Nance said.

"Well, who was it, then?" Lizzy asked, her tone a challenge.

"The feller I met said he was from Tennessee," Nance said.

"Come on," Birch said to Lizzy. He took her hand and helped her up onto his horse. "We'll go see Fincher."

As they rode away Nance leaned over the edge of the porch and spat out her snuff juice.

Lizzy buried her face in the back of Birch's flannel shirt. "Poor little Roberta," she said. "I've heard her crying every night since Mama took her off, begging to come home. I can't stand it anymore, Birch. I've got to know where she is."

Birch just rode along and said nothing. It was a sunny afternoon. The dogwoods were beginning to blossom and there was greenery everywhere. The following Sunday would be Easter. Lizzy's pregnant belly was warm against him.

"Will thinks she's yours, Birch," Lizzy said. "And maybe she should have been."

In an hour and a half they rode down the little trail to the Reverend Fincher's cabin. Two nasty children were playing in the yard, one chasing the other with a stick. The reverend was in a chair on the porch, his big leather Bible open on his knees.

"Howdy," Birch said.

"Good afternoon," the reverend said. "Can I help you folks?"

"Reckon you'd be Reverend Fincher?" Birch asked.

"That's me. And you're the Phillips boy that runs the store."

"Yes sir. Uh, this woman here is looking for her little daughter. Did an old woman give you a little girl to raise?"

"My old woman's give me two younguns to raise already," the reverend said. "That's them there." A flicker of humor passed across his face and disappeared.

"This was a little blond girl, two and a half years old," Lizzy said.

"No sir, no sir. But I do recall meeting an old woman with a child about a month ago. I give them a ride this far up the mountain. She allowed as how she was aiming to take the child across the mountain to the county home. I said I didn't think the home would take a child. Then she offered her to me." He looked closely at Lizzy. "Was she yourn?"

Lizzy nodded and hid her face in her hands.

"Looks like you're fixing to have another one," the reverend said. "I explained to the woman that I already had as many kids as I could care for. Have you been to the home?"

"Yep," said Birch, looking down and rubbing his chin.

"So you don't know where the child is?"

"No."

"I let her and the little girl off where my road starts, and she seemed intent on going over the mountain. I reckon I should have done something."

"Wasn't your fault," Birch said. "She must have give it to somebody else."

"Weren't nobody else up in here that day, that I know of," the reverend said. "Won't you and your wife come in the house and have something to eat?"

"Better get on," Birch said.

"I'll pray for you both, and for the child," the reverend said. "I hope you find her. Why did the old woman take the child off, if you don't mind me asking?"

"We're poor," Lizzy sobbed. "We're so poor. We don't have nothing."

Birch turned the horse and they rode off. The reverend watched them go, shaking his head.

On their way back through Jonathan's Creek they passed the Hatley place. Cora Hatley saw them through the kitchen window and came out onto the back porch.

"Birch? Lizzy?" she hollered. "I heard you've lost little Roberta. You ain't found her yet?"

"No, ma'am," Lizzy said. "Not yet."

"I sure hope you find her," Mrs. Hatley said, wiping her hands on her apron.

Birch nudged his horse on down the trail. After they were out of earshot of Mrs. Hatley Lizzy asked, "How did she know about it? Does everybody on Jonathan's Creek know about it?"

"Everybody in Haywood County knows about it," Birch said.

As they drew near the Putnam cabin Lizzy gripped Birch's arm tightly. "Will's home," she said. "Just let me off here. Thank you so much, Birch. I hate dragging you into this."

"I hate things have turned out this way, Lizzy," Birch said. He helped her down. She took his hand and kissed it and turned and walked to the cabin. Birch rode off toward his home.

As Lizzy climbed slowly up the porch steps Will came out and stared at her.

"Where you been?" he asked.

"Hunting little Roberta," she said.

He grabbed her shoulders and shook her. "You got to give it up! You got a family. You got me, and you got another baby on the way. You got to forget her."

"Get away from me!" she sobbed, and pushed him. He slapped her mouth and it bled.

She went to the edge of the porch and picked up a hoe and came back and swung it at him.

"Hey!" he said. "Goddamnit, quit!"

She swung it again and hit him on the side of the head and he toppled off the porch into the dirt.

In a few seconds he picked himself up and touched the

side of his head and then looked at his own blood on his fingers. Then he went to the side of the house and puked.

On the porch Lizzy was still holding the hoe. Behind her was Nance, a twig in her mouth. Will laughed a silly, uncertain little laugh and went over to the pump and washed his face and head.

Just after noon on Monday, April 7, 1913, Will and old Joe were sitting on the porch after a scant meal of corn-meal mush and some milk that Will had brought back from the Ledford place. Nance was washing the dishes and Lizzy was helping as best she could. Jane was sick in bed.

Joe saw two riders coming down the Indian trail. He strained to see who they were. "Who is that, son?" he asked.

"Looks like Deputy Jack Carver and Dave Leather-wood," Will said.

Deputy Jack dismounted and tied his horse to the maple tree in the yard. Dave just sat in his saddle. Jack had brought Dave along because he knew how hotheaded Will Putnam could be. He thought he might need some help.

"Howdy, Jack," Joe said. "Come up on the porch and talk."

"How you doing, Joe? Will?"

"Fine, fine," the Putnam men said.

Jack leaned against one of the logs that served as roof

braces. "I need to talk to Nance and Lizzy about something," he said.

Lizzy came outside and eased herself into a chair, and then Nance came out and leaned against the doorframe.

"Well, it looks like you got some explaining to do, Nance," Jack said. "People are talking a lot about this situation, and they've come to me. I got to do something about it."

Lizzy started to cry. Nance leaned and spat off the porch.

"Some folks say you gave the little girl, Roberta, to the county home. But I checked, and she ain't there. Others say you gave her to Reverend Fincher, that lives up on Utah. But then others say you gave her to a man in black, in a black buggy. What's the straight of it, Nance?"

"Ain't nobody's business," Nance said. "Ain't nobody's business what we done with our own youngun. She was ourn. We could do what we wanted to."

Lizzy held her apron up to her face.

"Now, Nance," Jack said, "I'm afraid it ain't as simple as that. There's laws saying what you can do and what you can't. Now, Mrs. Cora Hatley says you come by her house that morning, February twenty-sixth, and you told her you was taking the child to the county home. And then you come back about noon without the child. But you didn't have time to go to the county home and back by noon."

"A man give me a ride," Nance said, "and I give her to him."

"Well, Nance, I talked to Reverend Fincher. He gave you a short ride, he says, and he says you offered him the little girl. But he didn't take her."

"Must have been that other feller," Nance said. "Had a bunch of pots and pans in his wagon. Said he was from Tennessee." She spat off the porch again.

Lizzy began to cry harder.

"Your story don't hold water, Nance. You've told it too many ways." Jack took his hat off and wiped the sweat from his brow with his sleeve. "That telephone of mine has gone crazy as hell over this. One person told me you cut that baby up into pieces and fed it to Jase Ledford's hogs. Another one said you sacrificed it to the devil. The community is hot about this, Nance, and wants to know what's happened to the child."

"Suspicions don't add up to a damn, Jack," Will said. "You got to have proof."

"I figure you all know what happened," Jack said. "So Nance and Lizzy and Will—you all are under arrest."

"Me?" Will said, outraged. "That ain't right! I didn't do nothing! It was Nance that done it. I didn't have nothing to do with it."

"I'm taking you in on suspicion. You and Lizzy are witnesses, if not accomplices."

Will stood up, his fists on his hips. "You ain't taking me nowhere," he said.

Jack eased his Colt .44 revolver out of his holster and aimed it at Will and cocked it.

"Wait!" Lizzy hollered. "We'll go!"

Behind Jack, Dave Leatherwood had cocked his Winchester and was looking at Will very solemnly. Sweat broke out on Will's face.

"Okay," he said. "You've got us in a bunch of trouble now, old woman," he said to Nance.

Chapter Fourteen

On the morning of Monday, April 14, 1913, Nance was finishing her breakfast in her jail cell, sopping her biscuits in a last bit of egg yolk. Will and Lizzy had finished their meals and Will had gone back to sleep on his cot.

When the food was all gone Nance sat with her arms folded looking through the bars at the sky. It was a fine spring morning and there were birds all around. Nance felt good and began to hum a little tune to herself.

"You oughtn't to be singing, old woman, in the spot you're in," someone said.

Nance looked around and saw the first curiosity seeker of the day. This one was a nasty, grubby little man, pale and skinny and unshaven, with a felt hat that had grease spots on it and a pair of worn-out overalls and no shirt.

"They's some people that wants to stretch your neck, old lady," he went on, grinning. "When they find that poor little girl where you put her, that'll be the end of you. Your game will be up."

"Go away," Lizzy said. "Please. We ain't done you no harm."

"I aim to be there when they hang this old crow," the grubby man said. "People can't tolerate what she done. She'll be made a example of. And I aim to see it. I seen a nigger hung one time. He cried and hollered and pissed on hisself, hee-hee! I ain't never seen a woman hung, not in sixty years. I've heard about you, old lady. People know about your evil powers. But the Bible says not to suffer one of your kind to live."

"Go away!" Lizzy shouted, waking Will up. "You nasty old man, you'll go to hell talking that way! You'd better hush your stupid old mouth!"

"Hee-hee!" the old man laughed. He had three teeth on his bottom gum and none on the upper.

By noon there were eight or nine people outside

Nance's cell, talking to her and taunting her and threatening her. Nance ignored them and sat staring at the wall, chewing on a twig, even when one moronic boy in dirty overalls threw a piece of brick through the bars, barely missing her. It shattered on the stone floor.

"Oh!" Lizzy hollered a moment later. "Oh!" She grabbed Nance's arm. "It's coming, Mama!"

She lay back on her cot and the little crowd saw a stain spread out underneath her. Will had his face pressed between the bars that separated him from the women.

"She's having her baby!" somebody hollered, and the crowd pressed against the bars. There were two teenage boys among them and they sniggered and watched. In just a short time the baby came. Will wiped his pocketknife on his shirt and handed it to Nance.

Deputy Jack had left Dave Leatherwood in charge of the search and was back in town early to take care of some paperwork. When he got to the courthouse he had to push his way through the crowd at the jail.

"Hey!" he said. "You people need to get out of here and go home. This old lady ain't no damn bear in a cage."

He was stunned to see Nance holding up a bloody infant boy with one hand and an open knife with the other.

"Nance! Hold it!" he said, and pulled his Colt revolver.

Nance looked at him. The baby was crying. She figured out what Jack was upset about and handed the knife back to Will, who was grinning. Jack, embarrassed, holstered his pistol.

Nance gave Lizzy the baby. Lizzy was crying and groaning.

"My God," Jack said. "Somebody go for a doctor."

"Ain't no need for one now," Nance said. She put a pinch of snuff between her gum and bottom lip. Jack wiped his mouth and felt faint.

"Go get Doc Crawford," he said to one of the boys in the crowd. "And the rest of you people, you don't need to be in here. Go on. Go on home."

The onlookers left the courthouse and took up their vigil on the lawn beneath Nance's cell window. Now and then one would holler, "You're going to hell, old woman!" or "You're gonna get hung, old witch!" and so on.

That evening Deputy Jack opened the cell door. "I want to talk to you, Lizzy," he said. She was worn out but she gave Nance the baby and went with Jack to his office.

"Lizzy," Jack said, sitting down at his desk, "I've been authorized to release you and Will, on one simple condition. That you have to sign this." He held out a single piece of paper covered with handwriting. "It just says what you and Will told me."

Lizzy read the page. It said simply that Nance had left with Roberta on the morning of February 26 with the understanding that she would take the child and herself to the county home, and that she had returned alone in about five hours.

She signed it.

"I need Will to sign it, too," Jack said.

Lizzy remained seated while he went back to the jail.

When Will came in with Jack he flashed a look at Lizzy. She was looking at the floor.

"Sign this and you can both go home," Jack said, handing the page to Will.

"I can't read this," Will said, standing with his hip thrust out. He tossed the page at Jack's desk and it fluttered down.

"Read it to him, Lizzy."

She read it out with no difficulty, though she was weak and in pain. Will ran his fingers through his hair and took Jack's pen and scratched a mark about the length of a name under Lizzy's signature. Then Jack gave them their personal articles.

"Dave Leatherwood will take you home in his wagon," he said. "Don't leave the county. There'll be a trial and you're both witnesses."

"Thank you, Jack," Lizzy said. Will said nothing. Then they left.

On Utah Mountain the searchers had started home. The search was a week old now.

"I don't figure she's up there," Frank Janes was saying to Lois Ransom and Aaron Hatley. "I figure a bear's done got her and eat her. I don't figure we'll find her at all."

"If we don't find a body the solicitor can't prosecute, that's what my daddy says," Lois said.

"There won't be no trial," Frank said. "I've heard people talking. They're gonna lynch old Nance. You mark my words."

"There won't be no proof against her if there ain't a

body," Aaron said. "Nobody can prove she done nothing to the child. So how can they lynch her?"

"You watch, short-life. They'll drag her old ass right out of the courthouse and take her to that big oak on the hill above town. People's been hung on that tree before. They don't need no proof. I know she done it, and you know it, and everybody knows it. I aim to help them out."

Aaron looked at Lois. He didn't want to see a lynching, and neither did she, he could tell. He loved her so much. She had something, a lovable quality that a lot of mountain girls didn't have. She was skinny and buck-toothed, but she had sense.

Not like Laurie Jean Bramlett.

When they reached the wagons Aaron and his father got in theirs and Frank and Peedro climbed in with the Ransoms because Frank lived in their direction. Aaron saw him scoot over close beside Lois, jabbering his stupid nonsense. He knew Lois was too smart to fall for Frank's banter. But he'd thought that about Laurie Jean, too.

Aaron wondered as he rode home with his father whether he might somehow kill Frank and make it look like an accident. He could take him hunting and shoot him accidentally on purpose, or stick a hunting knife into him and claim he fell on it. But then he'd be in the same fix as old Nance Dude. Aaron knew he couldn't get away with something like that. Nobody ever did.

Chapter Fifteen

By the tenth day of the search many people had begun
to doubt whether the child would be found at all, but
their fury at Nance did not abate. They were still sure
that Nance had done away with her granddaughter. The
question was how.

On Friday, April 18, only about fifteen people showed up at the foot of the mountain. Among them were Aaron Hatley and his father, and Lois Ransom and her father, and Frank Janes and his dog, Peedro, and Jase Ledford and Joellen, and Birch Phillips. And of course Deputy Jack Carver and Dave Leatherwood and a few more.

The morning's search was unproductive, and the searchers all walked down to the lawn at Jonathan's Creek Baptist Church and ate the fried chicken that some of the womenfolk had prepared.

After their meal Lois and Aaron went back up the side of the mountain.

"Have you ever seen a dead person?" Lois asked.

"Yep," Aaron said. "Lots of times."

"When?"

"When my Grandpaw Caldwell died I seen him laying in the house, in a casket. Everybody said he looked real natural, just like hisself, but there was rouge on his cheeks that looked fake. He looked like a doll, or a statue. People brought chicken and my Aunt Hazel brought chocolate cake. I never tasted nothing as good."

"Why do people bring chicken and stuff?" Lois asked. "And mashed potatoes?"

"So the family won't have to cook," Aaron said, feeling intelligent and deep. "Have you ever seen one?" he asked Lois. "A dead person?"

"No."

They heard soft laughter behind them.

"Quick!" Lois said, and took Aaron's hand and led him

into some bushes. "Cover up," she said, and they got down in the leaves and scooped handfuls up over them until they were completely covered.

The laughter drew closer and Aaron could barely see Joellen and Birch coming around the mountain path. Aaron knew what Lois was up to. It was wicked mischief, not the sort of thing he expected of her at all. But it was too rich to pass up.

When Joellen and Birch were right beside them, Lois rose up slowly from the leaves, like the dead coming to life, and went "*Oooeeooo!*" like a ghost. And then Aaron did the same.

Birch and Joellen froze in their tracks and then Joellen ran off down the trail squeaking like a mouse.

Birch had his rifle cocked before he saw who the ghosts really were. He dropped the rifle and took off after the kids, who were shrieking with laughter. Birch caught them and when Joellen heard the laughter she stopped and came back up the trail. Birch started to laugh, too, but not Joellen, who commenced a pithy little lecture on the mortal dangers of childish behavior.

The searchers went all the way to the western ridge of the mountain, still following Deputy Jack's original plan. They were really just going through the motions, except for Frank Janes, who was still excited in his simpleminded way.

Aaron trudged along beside Lois and her father. He poked at the leaves next to the trail with a dead hickory limb. He had decided that old Nance might really have given the little girl away to some traveler who would never be seen again.

"If we don't find little Roberta, what will the law do with Nance?" Aaron asked Mr. Ransom.

"What they call the burden of proof is on the prosecution," Mr. Ransom said. "That means she don't have to prove she's innocent. The solicitor has to prove she's guilty. With no body, I can't see how they can do that."

Up ahead Frank Janes went over the crest of Utah and down about a hundred feet onto a big granite knob that stuck out from the mountainside. Peedro went right to a place where there were rocks piled up and began to scratch and whine.

"Come on, Peedro," Frank called, but the dog seemed determined to dig at the rocks. Frank whistled and clicked his tongue but Peedro kept scratching and whining so Frank made his way out onto the ledge in front of the rocks. It struck him for the first time that they looked as if someone had piled them up on purpose. He took hold of one of them and pulled at it. It came loose and three or four other rocks rolled away.

The smell hit him and disoriented him for a moment but then it dawned on him what he had found. He realized he had better be sure and not make a fool of himself. He breathed through his mouth and strained to move a large rock so that he could see back into the cleft.

It was four o'clock and the light from the afternoon sun fell upon a little ball of blond hair.

"Oh, God! It's her! It's her! I see her! Oh, God!" Frank

hollered, breaking into sobs. He almost fell from the ledge in his horror and ecstasy.

Aaron and Lois and Mr. Ransom were at the top of the ridge. They couldn't see Frank but they could hear him. They looked at one another and grinned. Aaron made his way down the bank to the knob, anxious to show Frank Janes up for the pretentious fool he was.

"It's her, it's her! Right there she is," Frank was saying and wiping his eyes. "Dear Jesus, it's little Roberta Putnam."

Suddenly Aaron believed him. He scrambled out onto the ledge. He thought later how odd it was that the rocks looked normal and natural at first, and then when he looked at them another way another aspect popped out, like a face in woodgrain. They had been piled up by somebody.

Aaron saw the look on Frank's face, but he wanted to see, too, and so he pulled away another rock and looked in.

She was lying on her face in a pile of damp, dark leaves, her blond hair still beautiful as only a child's can be. She had on a lot of dresses and the one on top was one Aaron had seen his sister Margaret wear when she was small.

Then the smell assaulted him and he saw her thin little legs and bare feet all blackened, and her hands blue and purple. The ends of her fingers were gone, with nothing left but little stumps caked with month-old blood.

Beside her in the leaves was the whimmy diddle he

had made for Margaret. Aaron rocked backwards and
passed out.

He came to fifty feet down the side of the mountain,
in a little grassy place. Deputy Jack and Lois and Lot
Ransom were looking down at him. They helped him up
but he was unsteady on his feet. He went over into the
trees and puked until his stomach was empty.

"Somehow I felt like harm was going to come to that
child," Cora Hatley said at home that night. "Her feet
was bare and there was bags under her little eyes. And
she would cough. She tried to smile . . ." Mrs. Hatley
wiped her eyes and went on. "She tried to smile at me
when Nance asked if we wanted her. And Nance smiled,
too. If I had ahold of that old woman I'd kill her right
now! I'd choke her to death with these two hands, as God
is my witness!"

She held up her hands, and Aaron saw wrinkles in
them he had never noticed before.

The world didn't seem right to Aaron for a long while
after that. He felt afraid of everything, especially the
dark. In the dark he would see old Nance Dude's face,
and his mother's hands, and dead and decayed little
Roberta Putnam, and it was all he could do to keep from
crying out.

Chapter Sixteen

Nance was charged with first-degree murder the day after the coroner's jury met. When the story came out in the *Clarion* more than a hundred people showed up at the courthouse to gawk at her. A photographer took a few pictures of Nance while she sat looking down at her rawboned hands with a kind of grim resignation. She knew she'd done the wrong thing, and been caught at it.

"Hang the old witch!" somebody outside hollered, right under the barred window of her cell.

Nance was alone now, since Deputy Jack had let Lizzy and Will go home. Lizzy had promised she would come and visit, but so far she hadn't. Nance had been more or less alone all her life, though, so she wasn't afraid.

Deputy Jack went out onto the steps of the courthouse and squared his shoulders. "Neighbors!" he said loudly.

"Give us that old woman!" a man hollered. "We'll do right by her."

"Neighbors," Jack said. "This is no way for Christian people to act. The law will deal with her."

"The law's too good for her!" some woman shouted.

"Did she have help?" another person hollered.

"Not as we know of," Jack said. "She's been charged with first-degree murder, and she'll be tried. If she's found innocent she'll be let go, and if she's found guilty she'll be electrocuted. That's the law, and I'm sworn to uphold it. I put my hand on the Bible and give my word. And if that means I have to deal with some of you that want to take the law into your own hands, well then by God I'll deal with you."

"Why'd she do it?" somebody asked.

"Yeah, why? Is she a witch?" a man shouted.

"I reckon we'll find out at the trial," Jack said. "Now you all go on home."

Among the people in the crowd were Aaron Hatley and his father. They didn't want to see a lynching, but they'd never witnessed such a pitch of excitement in their lives. Since he'd seen little Roberta's body Aaron couldn't help feeling that Nance deserved whatever she got.

The next edition of the *Clarion* carried a letter:

The Murdered Baby

Haywood's citizenship, even to the very lowest class, stands appalled at the brutal, barbarous, fiendish murder of little Bonnie Roberta Putnam. The unspeakable horror and nameless atrocity of the crime against innocence and against our fair mountain land make the hardest heart throb with a sensation of pain and humiliation.

A pitiable and tragic picture presents itself. A little child—the incarnation of trust and innocence, the personification of all that is pure and good in the world, the embodiment of helplessness and dependency—turned out of its rightful home into the wide, cold world and being led away in its childish happiness and glee all ignorant of its impending doom. And think of the little one alone on the mountain, penned in with rocks like a wild beast, suffering untold agonies through the terrors of darkness and cold and storm—hungering, thirsting, freezing—crazed with fright—and crying till its little heart was broken, begging in its baby prattle for help—with nothing to answer its cry save the melancholy sigh of the night wind. Not a picture of man's even-handed inhumanity to man, but the diabolical vengeance of superior strength over a helpless child. Is it not strange that remorse itself did not unlock the hardened, inhuman heart, and is it not strange that the demon hand that so ruthlessly sealed the liberty and life of this little one did not unbend to the pleadings of conscience and come with the dawn of a new day bringing with it comfort and freedom? We can only think with horror of the help that never came—and we can also think of a thousand friends that would have gladly rushed up the mountain side in the depth of a winter's night had they only heard that baby's cry.

But the dreary hours, freighted with most of the agonies that come to human beings through a life-time, crept over this little sufferer, so faint and sick with no hand to minister to her, and we can see her languishing, perishing, dying—with her defenseless head pillowed upon a powerless arm in a vain attempt to hide her face from her fears, and doubtless wondering to the last with a baby's reason why she was thus forsaken. How good that she was able to do that one only thing left to her—to die, and we can only hope that a pitying God speedily put an end to her tortures.

But it was only a baby you say! Yes, only a baby—

whose little hands had harmed no one—whose little lips had spoken ill of none—only a baby, whose little life had brought no evil influences into other lives—yes—only a baby with a baby's feeling—weeping, starving, homeless, friendless, deserted, dying alone upon a mountain top—but where God was near and where death was sweet.

Another picture presents itself. A little child, transfigured and ascending into Heaven. Only a baby—yet glorified and in Paradise! Whose anguish of body and soul was soothed with the indescribable peace of Heaven, whose tears were dried, and whose every want was fed by the bountiful hand of Him who tenderly said "of such is the kingdom of Heaven."

Mrs. W. T. Crawford

A week went by while Nance sat in jail. Lizzy finally came to visit and brought little Robert Louis with her.

"I guess I'll die in jail," Nance said.

"Some people say you won't be convicted, Mama," Lizzy said. "They say a old woman like you couldn't have lifted them big rocks by yourself."

Nance just sat quietly. She knew how people felt. She knew they wanted to hang her.

"You got to look on the bright side, Mama," Lizzy went on. But she didn't really know what the bright side was.

"Did you bring me some snuff?" Nance asked.

"Yes, Mama. Right here. Oh, and Preacher Rabb's wife come by yesterday and brought you some dresses. Look at this one." Lizzy pulled a dark green dress out of a flour sack.

"It's real nice," Nance said. "I reckon I'll wear it tomorrow."

"Do they still feed you good, Mama?"

"It's not as good as home-cooked, but they's plenty of it. I can't eat it all."

"Are you sleeping good?"

"Yep. Ain't had no trouble."

"That's good. Oh, old Jase Ledford come down to the house yesterday evening. He said we could skip the rent this month. It's just as well. We couldn't have paid him anyway. There's still barely enough for the four of us. Will just lays around. It's time he was helping Billy with the planting. But he's got a lot of pride, you know."

"If they convict me they'll hang me, or electrocute me," Nance said.

"They won't do that. They'd never do that to a poor old woman."

"If they don't I guess I'll die in prison."

Little Robert Louis started to fuss and cry so Lizzy unbuttoned her dress and stuck her nipple into his mouth. An old man in the next cell stared bleary-eyed.

"That old feller looks like he wants him a little titty milk, don't he, Robert Louis?" Lizzy asked. She was trim and pretty again after having the baby, and was even cheerful. She knew very well that her little girl had been murdered and her mother was in jail for it. But life had to go on. It was Nance who had taught her that. Deep inside she knew old Nance was a survivor.

———————

The next court convened May 6 so Nance was in jail until then. She never talked to anybody except Lizzy and her lawyer, Ted Howell. Howell was a young man the court had appointed. He came to talk to Nance an hour before the trial.

"What you've got to do, Mrs. Hannah," he said, "is plead insanity. Then they'll put you in an asylum, which is not near as bad as prison. Or getting electrocuted."

"I ain't crazy," Nance said. "And anyway I didn't do it. I give that child to a feller in a buggy."

Howell threw up his hands in exasperation.

When the trial started Deputy Jack led Nance into the courtroom and set her down beside Howell at a table on the right of the judge and opposite the solicitor, Felix Alley. Lizzy and her baby found a place on the front-row bench behind Nance.

Judge Garland S. Ferguson entered from his chambers, behind the bench. He had never seen a courtroom so packed, so threatening. He motioned for Deputy Jack.

"What the hell is going on here?" the judge asked.

"They want to see old Nance strung up."

"Nothing like that will happen in my circuit," the judge said. "Have you got the jurors? How many did you call?"

"I called seventy men," Jack said. "We'll need that

many to find twelve that ain't already set on stringing her up today."

Judge Ferguson rapped his gavel and the crowd settled down to a low growl. "Nancy Ann Hannah," he proclaimed, "you are charged with the murder of Roberta Putnam by starvation and exposure. How do you plead?"

"My name ain't Hannah," Nance said. "It's Kerley."

The judge peered at her over his glasses.

"I was married to Howard Kerley," she mumbled. Her arms were folded and she had a matchstick in her mouth. She was looking down.

"Please take that match out of your mouth, Mrs. Kerley, and speak up. Now, how do you plead?"

"Not guilty, Your Honor," Ted Howell said.

The crowd stirred, but the judge looked at them sternly and they quieted down.

"Let's get on with jury selection, then," the judge said. "Wallace Ammons?"

A big-eared man in dirty overalls got up from the first row. "Come up here," the judge said. The man came and sat down in the big oak chair on the judge's left.

Solicitor Alley walked up to him. "Wallace, where do you live?" he asked.

"Waynesville, Mr. Alley, sir."

"Do you know the defendant, Nancy Ann Kerley?"

"Everybody calls her Nance Dude," Wallace said, and a general chuckle came from the crowd.

"You know her?" Alley asked again.

"Yes sir. She murdered that little girl."

"Acceptable," Alley said.

"Unacceptable," Ted Howell said. "For cause."

"You may step down," the judge said. The crowd murmured.

"Samuel Anders," the judge called, and Anders came up and sat down. He needed a haircut and his shoes were caked with mud.

"Do you know the defendant?" Alley asked the man.

"Yes sir, I do. She buried that baby in the rock cleft."

"Acceptable," Alley said.

"Unacceptable," Ted Howell said.

The courtroom buzzed. "Ain't nobody acceptable?" one man hollered out.

The judge looked at Deputy Jack and at the crowd and whacked his gavel. "I'll clear this courtroom if you all don't be quiet," he said. "We're just picking a jury, that's all. We want jurors that are acceptable to both the prosecution and the defense. This woman will get a fair trial here. Now be quiet."

The courtroom quieted down but the judge had an idea of what he was up against. They—Judge Ferguson, Alley and Howell—went through ten more men and came up dry. The judge then called the two lawyers to the bench.

"We're getting nowhere with this, Judge," Alley said. "Everybody in the whole damn county knows about her and what she did."

"Can't you accept any of these people, Mr. Howell?" the judge asked.

"I can't let my client be tried by a bunch of people that have her convicted in their hearts already," Howell said. "This case ought to be moved somewhere else."

The judge shook his head. "Look. These hillbillies just want out of sitting on a jury, that's all it is."

"I'd be a sorry lawyer if I let these people try my client, Judge," Howell said. "They want to string her up on that big oak tree outside town. I've heard them talking about it. You've got to change the venue on this case."

The judge sent the lawyers back and then pounded his gavel. The courtroom got quiet. "The case of the State versus Nancy Ann Kerley is hereby remanded to the judicial district of Swain County," he said. "Court is adjourned until nine o'clock tomorrow."

The reaction the judge expected came immediately. The courtroom exploded into a roar.

"Ain't you going to try her?" some woman squawked. "What's the damn law good for?"

"She buried that baby alive! Jail's too good for her!" a man shouted.

"Hang her, hang her!" several people called while the judge kept banging his gavel.

A tall man in overalls, his long johns showing, jumped over the back of the bench in front of him and grabbed Nance's sweater and pulled her backwards until her chair toppled over. "I got her, I got her!" he yelled.

Lizzy put little Robert Louis down on the bench beside her and jumped up and went flailing into the man, but then two more people joined the fight, and then half a dozen more. Two women held Lizzy while several men dragged Nance down the aisle toward the door.

Deputy Jack saw what they were about to do. He pulled his .44 and tried to make his way through the crowd, which was pouring out into the street.

The judge was screaming at Jack, "Stop them, stop them!"

A man grabbed Jack's gun hand and another grabbed him around the neck. Jack was a powerful man, but they wrenched the gun away and held him as the mob made its way up the street toward the oak tree on the hill. There were a hundred angry people, with Nance right in the middle. Her face and hair were bloody. Far behind was Lizzy, whom the women had turned loose. She was screaming at them to stop, to wait.

The mob pulled Nance along until they reached the oak tree. There was a low-hanging limb that had been used for hangings before. Someone produced a hemp rope.

Then suddenly before them appeared two men on horseback who rode directly into their midst and pulled up short in front of the men holding Nance.

"Turn her loose," said the first rider, who was Jase Ledford. "Turn her loose or I'll kill you."

He cocked his pistol and aimed it at one of the men holding Nance. The second rider, Dave Leatherwood, said nothing but cocked his .30-30 rifle and aimed it at the face of the man holding the noose. The mob turned

Nance loose and she staggered and fell on the ground. She looked up at Jase, not comprehending.

Deputy Jack pushed through the mob, which was taking on an overall sheepish look. His left arm was limp and his face was twisted in anger and pain and he was sucking air through clenched teeth. He helped Nance to her feet and led her through the crowd and back down the street toward the jail.

Chapter Seventeen

Lizzy carried Robert Louis with her to the Ledford mansion and knocked on the big front door and waited. After a minute old Billy opened the door. He was gray now, and frail.

"I'd like to see Miss Joellen," Lizzy said.

"Come in, Miss Lizzy," the old black man said. She went in and sat on a little bench beside the door. Billy went up the spiral staircase and Lizzy could hear him speaking in low tones to Joellen.

Joellen came down the stairs. "Lizzy, what can I do for you?"

Lizzy stood. "Miss Joellen, I wouldn't bother you but you're the only person I know of who can help. You've done so much, I mean your daddy . . ."

"I'll be glad to help, really I will," Joellen said, and took Lizzy's free hand in hers. "Oh," she said, "this must be little . . ."

"Robert Louis."

"Like Robert Louis Stevenson. He's one of my favorite authors."

"Mine, too. I love to read, when I get a chance. But that's why I need your help, Miss Joellen. Mama's lawyer in Bryson City, over in Swain County, he says it might help Mama if somebody wrote a nice letter to Judge Ferguson for her. You know, saying some good things about her and all."

"Why, of course, I'd be glad to, Lizzy," Joellen said.

"You might could say she's worked hard all her life and never had a chance. And she took Roberta with her over Cataloochee just last year, to try and find a place for them after . . . after things got so hard for us and all."

Joellen smiled and nodded as if she understood.

"And it was Will, he never loved little Roberta. He's the one that wanted Mama to take her off."

The baby was starting to cry and fuss.

"Don't worry, Lizzy," Joellen said. "I'll get that letter off tomorrow. Things will turn out all right. Why, you've got little Robert Louis now, and I'm sure things will work out fine."

Later that day Joellen wrote,

Dear Judge Ferguson:

Mrs. Lizzy Putnam has requested that I write this letter on behalf of her mother, Mrs. Nancy Kerley.

Mrs. Kerley has always been a church-going woman and has worked hard for the Putnam family with whom she dwelt. She did an admirable job of raising her daughter Lizzy after being burned out of house and home by Lizzy's father, who was a drunk and used to beat them both.

She helped care for little Roberta, having just returned with the child from Tennessee, where she tried without success to find a place for them.

It is my honest belief that Mrs. Kerley's character is not bad enough to commit murder. Whatever she did was done with the well-being of her family as its motivation. It is hoped that you will take these facts into consideration. And it should be pointed out that Mrs. Kerley is about 65 years old and is hardly what one might call a dangerous person. She has had a hard time in life, and what happened is not entirely her fault.

Sincerely,

Joellen Ledford
Teacher
Jonathan's Creek School
Haywood County

Joellen put her quill pen down and let her mind wander. It still wasn't clear to her *why* old Nance had done what she had. Joellen really didn't understand it at all.

She read over the letter, humming a pleasant little song she had heard at the Presbyterian church. Lucille came up behind her and saw her folding the letter and putting it into its envelope.

"Who are you writing to, Joellen?" she asked.

Joellen jumped. "Oh!" She hesitated a moment. "It's a boy I met in Raleigh."

"Better not let Birch find out about this boy! What's he like?"

"Just a boy. Birch has nothing to worry about."

———

Nance sat in jail in the Swain County Courthouse in Bryson City from May to July. Lizzy came to see her once and brought her some snuff and some apples and some wool yarn and knitting needles, but the sheriff wouldn't let her keep the needles. She sat most of the time with her hands in her lap and her feet flat on the floor and never said anything.

A few days before her trial date her new court-appointed lawyer came to see her in her cell.

"Mrs. Kerley?"

Nance looked up without speaking.

"I'm your new lawyer, Sam Black." He sat on the cot beside her and put his briefcase in his lap.

"That's fine," she said. "But I ain't crazy. I ain't pleading insane. I'm innocent."

Black gazed at her for a long moment until she looked down at her shoes. Then he opened his briefcase and took out some papers.

"I've talked to Ted Howell about your case, Mrs. Kerley," he said. "Now, you know you're innocent, and I know it, but that don't cut the ice. It's the judge and the jury we got to worry about. And here's how it stacks up. One, your daughter, Lizzy Putnam, and your son-in-law, Will Putnam, have signed sworn statements that you took the child off on the morning of February twenty-sixth and that you came back about five hours later, alone. Two, we have a sworn statement by Mrs. John Hatley that you stopped at her house with the child and tried to give it to her. Three, we have another sworn statement by Reverend Fincher that he gave you a short ride, amounting to about two miles, and that you tried to give the child to him. And then, four, Lizzy and Will Putnam say in their statements that you told them upon your return that you took the child to the county home, but, five, the manager of the county home, Miss Myrtle Fisk, denies ever seeing you or the child."

He watched Nance for a reaction but there was none.

"Six, when the child's mother, Lizzy Putnam—your daughter—found out that the county home didn't have her, you told her you'd given the child to Reverend Fincher. But in his statement he denies that. And people who know him estimate him to be a fine, honest man."

Nance spat some snuff juice into her spit-can.

Black rubbed his nose and went on, "Then, seven, a search party found the child's decayed body, sealed up, buried alive, left to die slowly and tortuously. *The tips of her fingers were eaten off, Mrs. Kerley!*"

Nance jumped.

Black allowed the anger to fade slowly from Nance's eyes, and then he said, "Mrs. Kerley, people get awfully upset about a thing like this. It calls into question our basic humanity—the thought of a grandmother so cruelly murdering her own daughter's child. They want to punish someone for cold-blooded murder. It *was* cold-blooded, you see, because whoever did it had a chance to think it over. It wasn't done in anger. At any time in the first two or three, maybe four, days, that person could have gone and set the child free. But they didn't, whoever it was. They let the child suffer and die slowly, going through a long, lonely hell on earth. That is called murder in the first degree, and the punishment for that in North Carolina is electrocution. They strap you into a big chair and send a jolt of electricity through you and you feel like you've been struck by lightning. You jump and jerk for a few minutes, you shit on yourself and then you die."

Nance sat looking down, her arms folded.

"But now, according to this nice letter Judge Ferguson showed me from Miss Joellen Ledford, daughter of the prominent farmer Jason Ledford, you are not a bad person. You didn't do it for meanness or because you were crazy, but because of your poverty. But, see, the jury, the people who will judge your case, they're mostly poor folks, too, and none of them has ever done anything like this. They will never believe you didn't do it, and they won't excuse you for being poor. They'll find you guilty, and the judge will send you to the electric chair."

Nance glanced up at him and from somewhere she produced a straw and put it between her teeth. Black reached out angrily and grabbed it from her mouth and threw it down. Then he waited a minute and calmly went on.

"Did somebody help you roll those rocks over the front of that cave?" he asked.

"I didn't have no help," Nance said.

"If you plead innocent the jury will convict you, Mrs. Kerley. The prosecutor has photographs of the rocked-up cave and of little Roberta Putnam lying on her face with her body discolored. The jury will convict you of first-degree murder and you will die in the electric chair."

"I give her to a feller. They can't prove I didn't."

"Mrs. Kerley, that jury won't believe you gave that child to the county home, or to Reverend Fincher, or to a skinny man in a buggy, or to Jesus on a mule, or to a rabbit riding a bear. You've told it too many ways. They are not going to have a reasonable doubt in their minds that you buried that child alive and let her die slowly."

He lit a cigarette and let his words sink in.

Nance looked straight ahead and sniffed. "So I ain't got a chance," she said.

"If you plead innocent you'll be tried. And if you're tried you'll be convicted. And if you're convicted you'll be electrocuted. You'll be the first woman executed in North Carolina in this century. Have you ever heard of Frances Silver, Mrs. Kerley?"

"No," Nance said.

"Back in 1835 she chopped her husband up with an ax and threw the pieces into the fireplace and burned them up. He was a grown man, not an innocent child. They hanged her."

They both sat awhile. Black finished his cigarette and ground it out on the floor.

"I ain't crazy," Nance said.

"I don't think you are either, Mrs. Kerley. I think if you plead not guilty by reason of insanity the jury'll reject it and you'll be in the same fix as if you'd pled innocent in the first place."

Nance looked down at her worn-out shoes. "I never done it for meanness," she said.

"How has the food been here?" Black asked.

"Not too bad."

"It's about the same in Central Prison in Raleigh," he said. "And you'll have to work. Probably for the rest of your life. If you live a long time you might get out on parole for good behavior. That would beat hell out of getting electrocuted, wouldn't it?"

"What am I supposed to do?" Nance asked.

"You didn't actually *plan* it, did you? I mean, you didn't take her out that morning *intending* to bury her in that cave, did you?"

"No."

"So what we'll do is plead you guilty of murder in the second degree. You'll get a long prison term. You agree to that?"

"Okay," Nance said. "But that don't mean I'm saying I done it."

Black looked at her blankly a moment and then nodded and left.

The court record from Swain County looked like this:

Oct. 18, 1913

State of North Carolina vs. Nancy Kerley

Murder

The plea of not guilty heretofore entered is withdrawn, and the defendant through her counsel tenders to the State a plea of guilty of murder in the second degree, which plea is accepted by the Solicitor with the approval of the Court.

It is therefore on motion of the Solicitor for the State ordered and adjudged by the Court that the defendant Nancy Kerley be confined in the State Prison at hard labor for a period of 30 years.

On Friday, October 25, 1913, Nance boarded a train to Raleigh in the custody of Deputy Ray Bolden of the Swain County Sheriff's Department. She carried all her belongings in a flour sack decorated with pink polka dots.

Bolden took her to the back corner of the last passenger car and they sat in silence for the six hours the trip took. Bolden knew all about the case, as did everyone in the mountains.

At the Raleigh station they met a muscular, uniformed woman with short blond hair who took custody of Nance.

"How about it, Nance," Deputy Bolden said, grinning. "Did you do it?"

"I'm as innocent as you are," Nance said, and spat on the ground.

Bolden winked at the blond woman, who smiled cynically and led Nance away to the prison wagon.

On Monday, October 30, 1913, the mailman handed Lizzy a letter:

Dear Mrs. Putnam,

I am sorry I could not do more to help your mother. She pled guilty to second-degree murder, as I advised, and was sentenced to thirty years at hard labor. I believe that if she had pled innocent and been tried she would have wound up being executed.

She was guilty, in my opinion, only of being impoverished to a point of such degradation and desperation that she believed that her own survival, and yours, depended upon the sacrifice of little Roberta.

I hope to God the day comes when nobody will be subjected to such a condition and reduced to such a state of dejection. What happened to your mother should not have happened in the twentieth century.

I admire your mother for her will and endurance. If she lives, she might be paroled in a few years.

If I can be of any help to you please write to me at the Swain County Courthouse.

I wish you well.

Sincerely yours,
Sam A. Black, Attorney

Lizzy read the letter to Will on the porch. Little Robert Louis, now six months old, played with a spool at her feet. Will yawned and stood up and walked down into the yard. The weather was pleasantly chilly and around the cabin the leaves of the trees had turned to blazing red and yellow. He looked back at Lizzy and then shoved his hands into his overalls pockets and turned away and took a deep breath. He was glad they were rid of the old woman. And Lizzy had her looks back now, so he didn't think so much about Joellen Ledford anymore.

The next evening was Halloween, and Lois and Aaron and Aaron's sisters, Margaret and Cindy, and Laurie Jean Bramlett dressed up in homemade costumes at the Hatley house and set off to terrorize the residents of Jonathan's Creek. Aaron and Laurie Jean were a little old to go trick-or-treating but they had the excuse of going along to look after the younger children.

Aaron was outfitted like a genie out of *The Arabian Nights*, with a towel around his head for a turban, and one of his mother's old, floppy blouses, and a wooden scimitar he'd made from a long splinter of pine and a small piece of kindling wood tacked to it for a hand guard.

Cindy, who was twelve, was dressed up like a fat Negro slave, with charcoal on her face and a flowery kerchief in her hair.

And Margaret, nine, had little paper wings sewn onto a pretty white dress and a harp made of sticks and strings.

Laurie Jean was a fairy, with a stick with a paper star

on it for a magic wand, and a tiara of her mother's in her hair, and a pretty, new dress with embroidered pastel flowers.

Lois had on an old blue polka-dot dress and a green sweater, and snuff in her mouth, and wrinkles drawn on her face with charcoal. She went around with her arms folded over her breasts.

"Who are you supposed to be?" Aaron asked.

"Nance Dude," she said, and giggled.

"Where's Frank?" Aaron asked Laurie Jean.

"He wouldn't come," Laurie Jean said, twirling around with her magic wand. "He says trick-or-treating is for kids."

Aaron was glad Frank wasn't coming. Frank always had to be the biggest show-off.

The first house they came to was the Putnams', and of course they didn't stop there. The next was the Ledford mansion. Aaron went up to the big door and knocked loudly. The sun was poised low in the sky, about to drop behind the mountains.

Lucille opened the door with Joellen right behind her. Lucille had a dazed, puzzled look on her face and obviously didn't realize what night it was. When she saw Lois looking like Nance her hand went up to her mouth and her eyes grew wide. "Oh?" she said.

"It's Halloween, Mother," Joellen said, laughing. "Come in, children."

She introduced them all to her mother and then went

to the pantry and brought them apples and nuts, which they stuffed into their pockets. Lucille looked at them as if they were wild animals escaped from a zoo.

The next house they went to was the Phillipses', right behind the general store, and Birch invited them into the store and gave them each a big sugar cookie and some cider, which they consumed on the spot.

By the time the sun went down they had reached the churchyard.

"Let's go see Roberta Putnam's tombstone," Lois said. Aaron could see her grinning wickedly in the moonlight.

"Let's don't," Margaret said.

"Don't be a scaredy-cat," Lois said. "Let's go, and I'll tell a witch story!"

"Okay," Aaron said, so the five of them walked past the church and among the tombstones. The moon was so bright they could read the inscriptions.

"There it is," Lois said, and they all went over to a little tombstone by the fence, all by itself. It said,

> Roberta Ann Putnam
> b. Nov. 15, 1910 d. Feb. 26, 1913
> The Rose of My Heart

Lois went right up and sat down on it, something none of the others would have done. Then she lit a tallow candle and held it in her lap. Behind her near the fence was an odd pile of old boards and limbs and brush. "Once upon a time," Lois began, and the rest of them gathered close. There was still a little mound of dirt where Roberta had been buried back in April.

"Once upon a time there was a poor farmer and his wife, and they had this little girl, Roberta."

"He was a woodcutter," Margaret piped in.

"I'm telling this," Lois said. "Now, they were so poor they didn't have enough to eat, and they had a old witch living with them. She was old and ugly and all wrinkled up and gray-headed, with snuff dripping out the side of her mouth." She let some snuff juice run out the corner of her lips and squinted one eye.

"Shoo!" Margaret said. Laurie Jean giggled.

"So one night the farmer tells the old witch to take the little girl off and leave her in the woods, so the rest of them would have enough to eat. But little Roberta, she overhears them and slips into the kitchen and gets her a cold biscuit."

"Because she was hungry," Margaret said to Cindy.

"No," Lois said. "It was 'cause she was smart. She puts the biscuit in her pocket and the next morning when the old witch takes her off into the woods she crumbles the biscuit up and scatters the crumbs behind her. That's so she can find her way back."

"But a bird eats them up!" Margaret blurted out.

"Shh! I'm trying to tell this. Now hush." Lois looked around her and cleared her throat. "So the old witch, she takes the poor little child up the side of this big, dark mountain, and she finds a little cave in the rocks, and she makes little Roberta crawl back into it. Little Roberta fights her but the old witch uses magic on her and makes her go back in the hole. Then the witch turns and says to some big rocks, 'Come up, come up, and cover her up!' And the rocks roll over and close up the cave."

"Where's the gingerbread house?" Margaret asked.

"There ain't no such thing," Lois said, perturbed. "Anyway, when the old witch gets home the mama asks, 'Where's my little girl?' and the old witch, she says, 'I give her to somebody.' But then in a few days . . ."

"A month," Aaron said.

"Damn it!" Lois said, but then composed herself and cleared her throat again, loudly, and went on. "But then the mama gets to looking for the little girl, and gets a whole bunch of people looking for her, too, and they look for days and days but they can't find her nowhere. Then the mama finds this little trail of breadcrumbs, and follows it along, and they lead up to this place where the rocks are piled up, *and she pulls the rocks away and . . .*"

"*Whoooooooo!*" a voice called out from behind Lois, and they all looked. The pile of boards and brush started to move and shake. Aaron's hair stood on end. Margaret and Cindy screamed and jumped up and ran through the tombstones toward the cemetery gate. Laurie Jean was shaking wildly, her hands over her mouth.

Up through the boards came a figure all in white. "Oooo," it moaned, "I'm a-coming to get youuu."

Aaron was petrified, but he wanted to protect Lois, who had jumped down in front of Roberta's tombstone.

"I'm a-going to killll youuu," the ghost moaned, and

suddenly Aaron recognized the voice, and then he realized that Lois and Laurie Jean were not trembling and crying, but laughing.

"Margaret! Cindy! It's okay!" he hollered, but they were long gone, around the church and down the trail toward home.

Aaron leaped over Roberta's tombstone and pushed the ghost down and jumped on it and began hitting its face. He knew very well that it was Frank Janes. The sheet Frank wore prevented him from fighting back, much to Aaron's delight, and Aaron went on pummeling his face.

"Stop!" Lois and Laurie Jean hollered together, and tried to pull Aaron off. "Stop, you'll kill him!" Laurie Jean said.

Aaron got up. Frank pulled the sheet away.

"Damn! You about beat me to death," he said.

Lois started giggling again but Aaron grabbed her arm. "You little witch!" he said, and shook her. "You planned up this whole thing, didn't you?"

"Yes," Lois said. She was no longer giggling, but crying.

"This is just the awfullest thing you've ever done," Aaron said. But then he looked at Frank, whose face was bruised and cut, and began to chuckle. Then they all laughed for a while and left the graveyard and went home.

Chapter Eighteen

When Birch and Joellen were married Nance had been in prison nearly eight months.

The first thing she learned at Central Prison was that all the prisoners were required to carry a Bible everywhere they went.

"A penitentiary is a place to be penitent," the warden said. "When you get out of here I want you to be truly sorry for what you've done."

And then the hard labor started. During the week the convicts, both men and women, were transported by rail to work on a dike along the Roanoke River. They rode there on Monday and came back to Raleigh on Saturday, still carrying their Bibles. Sunday they were allowed to rest and go to chapel, where a skinny, stern old preacher counseled them about how to please God: Work and repent.

The work on the dike was hard. They had to shovel dirt onto a conveyor that emptied into boxcars or, on the other end, shovel the dirt into a wooden framework built along the riverbank. It was a grinding, twelve-hour-a-day job.

To Nance it did not seem a bad life, even though every day she dug until she was worn out and then lay on her cot and slept like a dead woman. It was actually pretty much the way life had always been for her, only simpler. She didn't have to worry about her next meal, or her clothing, or shelter, or rent, or anything.

And the food was good, though some of her fellow prisoners complained. The prison farm raised cattle and hogs and vegetables and grain, so they had beef, pork, milk, cornbread, tomatoes, beans, squash, on and on.

People left her alone. She was so old they respected her, at least until they found out what she'd done, and then they stayed away from her. They could never get more than two words out of her. She took a piece of advice offered by Sam Black and kept to herself.

One evening in the stockade by the river a fat little woman named Wilma Bartlett, a Lumbee Indian, couldn't find her comb. It was a comb her daughter had given her, an expensive one, and Wilma was in a stew. Her chubby hands darted everywhere, feeling under mattresses, in purses, everywhere.

"Get up from there, Sue-Sue," Wilma said to a sullen young woman who was sprawled across her cot. Sue-Sue got up so Wilma could look under her mattress. Wilma did the same to three other women, and none of them put up any resistance. Then she came to Nance.

"Get up, old woman," she said.

"I ain't got it," Nance said.

"You better get up," Wilma said, furious.

Nance reached down beside her bunk and got her spit-can and spat into it.

"If you don't move so I can look, I'll move you," Wilma said.

"You ain't moving me," Nance said.

Wilma looked Nance in the eye. "What are you in here for, old woman? What'd you do?"

"Nothing," Nance said.

"I poisoned my mama and daddy," Wilma said. "You ain't got my comb, anyway."

"I got one," Nance said, and reached into her worn-out

flour sack and brought out a green shell comb with several broken teeth and showed it to Wilma.

"That ain't it," Wilma said. "But that's a pretty one."

"It ain't worth nothing," Nance said. "It's real old." She looked at it a moment, wondering where she had got it.

A torrent of memories assailed her, threatening to wash her away—Dude's arms around her that day at the old mill, and Howard's woeful face, and the hurt in Woody's eyes. Then she remembered. She'd found it under the bed in Dude's miserable little cabin, covered with years of dust and mold.

"It's pretty," Wilma said again, and went on with her search.

———

One day in December 1916 the guard handed Nance a letter. She took it to her bunk and turned it over and over for an hour or more. Then Wilma came in from the yard.

"Got you a letter?" Wilma asked. "Why don't you open it up?" Wilma never got any mail.

"Can't read," Nance said.

"I can read it to you," Wilma said. "If it ain't written in German or something."

Nance opened it and a ten-dollar bill fell out. She took the bill and looked at it and put it into one of her worn-out shoes. Then she handed the letter over and Wilma read it:

Dear Mama,

I hope you have a nice Christmas even though you are there in prison. I hope you know that I have never held nothing against you. We just had a lot of real bad luck.

I hope you will act good and be friendly to people there and not make no enemies. When I think of the kind of people you are in there with I want to cry. But I'm sure some of them are real nice and have just had some hard luck like you.

Jane died Sunday, November 28. She just quit breathing in her sleep. They said she was 70. She was a good old woman and never gave nobody no trouble. Old Joe don't even realize she's gone. He don't know anything anymore, he just sets on the porch and looks far away. Will has promised to marry me next June and I am so happy that little Robert Louis will not have to be called bad names and looked down on all his life. He is three now and is growing strong and Will is a pretty good daddy to him. The old rooster flogged him last Tuesday but didn't hurt him bad, just scared him. Maggie Phillips died three months ago.

Jase Ledford is not after his rent no more now that Will is working hard for old Billy and when he dies Will hopes Mr. Ledford will put him in charge.

Try to sleep and eat good and be nice to people and maybe we'll see each other again one of these days. Merry Christmas. In Christian love,

Your daughter Lizzy Putnam

Nance worked on the Roanoke River dike until it was finished in 1925. She and Wilma stuck close together until 1927, when Wilma died of cancer in the prison infirmary. She was sixty-one.

Then Nance went back to being her solitary self. She still worked, cleaning and mopping and washing and mending. She worked right up until the day she was paroled. The warden's secretary made this entry in the prison record book: "May 21, 1929, Nancy Kerley paroled in view of age of prisoner."

She had stayed in prison over fifteen years. When she got out she was eighty years old.

Back home on Jonathan's Creek Robert Louis Putnam was sixteen. Birch and Joellen Phillips now had two children, boys, both blond. And Aaron Hatley had married Lois Ransom and they had a son, Aaron, Jr.

Jase Ledford had died in 1926 of "natural causes," as the *Clarion* put it. Lucille had died in 1925. Old Joe Putnam had died way back in 1920. Frank Janes had been killed in a hunting accident in 1928. Old Judge Ferguson was dead, and Deputy Jack Carver was retired.

World War I was over. Aaron Hatley had served in France in the Eighteenth, or "Wildcat," Division and had come home safely except for losing his hearing in his right ear because of an exploding shell.

Many things remained the same on Jonathan's Creek. Birch still had the general store, and Joellen still taught school. Birch still made whiskey and sold it, though he was a little more cautious about it because of the Volstead Act of 1919. And old Reverend Colby Rabb still preached at the little Baptist church.

———————

Nance got off the train in Waynesville on Tuesday, May 22, 1929. She had a paper bag with her few things in it. At that time Aaron Hatley was working at Ashley's Department Store and studying the Bible. He was driving home from work in his worn-out car when he saw a little old woman walking along. He stopped beside her.

"Need a ride, ma'am?" he hollered. She looked at him and he saw that it was Nance Dude. She was toothless and totally gray and looked old as sin.

She said nothing but got in and closed the door. In her left hand were her Bible and her paper bag.

"Nance?" Aaron said.

"Going to Lizzy's place," she said.

"The Putnam place?"

"Yep."

She couldn't have weighed ninety pounds.

"How long you been gone, Nance?"

"Fifteen years."

Aaron supposed he had thought she was dead. But she wasn't. Here she was.

He drove her up to the Putnam cabin. There was nobody on the porch. Nance got out and shut the door, firmly for such a frail old woman. Aaron cut the motor off and waited for her to go into the house.

She hobbled up onto the porch and went to the door. She hesitated and then rapped with her aged knuckles.

Will opened the door and came out on the porch. "Nance? Is that you? They let you out?"

"Yep," she said, and looked down at her shoes.

"Mama?" Lizzy called, and came through the door. She grabbed Nance and hugged her. "Mama, Mama, I'm so glad to see you! Come on in the house."

"I'm looking for a place to stay," Nance said.

Will and Lizzy looked at each other. Will pinched his nose and shook his head. "Look, Nance, we don't hardly have no room for you," he said. Behind him a gangly boy—Robert Louis—came out onto the porch and looked curiously at his old grandmother.

Nance looked at Lizzy and Lizzy looked down at her hands and wiped them on her apron. "It's a awful small place, Mama," she said. "But we want you to come visit as much as you can. Can you stay for supper?"

"Got to go find me a place to live," Nance said. She held onto the doorframe and took off her left shoe and brought out a ten-dollar bill. "Here's your money. I don't need it," she said.

"No, no, Mama, please."

But Nance had put the money in Lizzy's hand and was climbing down the front steps. She hopped her way back to Aaron's car.

Aaron felt immediately that it was his fault they didn't take Nance in. If he'd just put her out and gone on they would have had to take her. Now she was his problem, he realized.

Nance opened the door and got in. She looked straight ahead. Aaron couldn't help staring at her. She was a kind of legend, and that made him start to want to help her out, to be part of her story somehow.

He drove her back down the road and stopped at Birch Phillips's store. Birch was nodding behind the counter when they went in. He jumped when he saw Nance, and Aaron laughed.

"See who I got here?" Aaron asked.

"Nance? Is that old Nance?"

Nance stood looking around, just a little old woman, lost and helpless.

"You need some snuff?" Aaron asked her, but she just stood looking at Birch.

"You come in on the train from Raleigh?" Birch asked her.

"Yep."

"You had anything to eat?"

"No."

Birch scratched his head. "You going back to live with Will and Lizzy?" he asked her.

"They ain't got room," Aaron said.

"Nothing to eat and noplace to stay," Birch said. Aaron was hoping Birch could come up with some answers.

"Is that a Bible?" Birch asked.

"Yep," Nance said. "Had to tote it around at the farm. Had to show you was sorry for what you done."

"You sorry for what you done, Nance?" Birch asked, and winked at Aaron.

"I reckon so. But I never done nothing," she said, and looked from Birch to Aaron and back to Birch again, frightened.

"Will and Lizzy won't take her in?" Birch asked, scratching his head. "Well, you know it might not be such a good idea for her to settle here again. Lots of people remember."

Aaron nodded and glanced at Nance, who looked like she wanted to scurry under a chair.

"I got a cousin, Ray, over in Bryson City that was telling me about a cabin on his property that nobody is living in," Birch said. "Said he might tear it down for the lumber. Reckon she could make it on her own? How old are you, Nance?"

"I ain't got no idea," Nance said.

"Well," Aaron said, "she was sent up, let's see, fifteen years ago, and she was about sixty-five then, as I recall. That'd make her eighty or so now."

Birch went into the storeroom and called his cousin in Bryson City while Nance and Aaron stood waiting. Then he came back out rubbing his chin. "He says it's still there. It's in a little settlement called Conley's Creek. He wants rent of five dollars a month. It's got water and a wood stove but no electricity."

"I don't need none of that electricity," Nance said. She had found a kitchen match to put into her toothless mouth.

Birch wrote directions to the cabin and Aaron took Nance home with him for the night.

"Look who I got with me!" he hollered to Lois.

Lois was fixing supper and came into the living room from the kitchen smiling expectantly. When she saw Nance she was rendered speechless. Nance looked like an aged little animal with frightened eyes. Like a badly mistreated stray cat.

Aaron persuaded Nance to sit in his easy chair and then he explained the situation to Lois. Aaron, Jr., came in from the backyard and stared at the curious old woman until Lois finished getting supper. Nance accepted a plate of green beans and a wedge of cornbread.

That night she declined to go to bed, which made Lois feel relieved. The next morning they found her asleep in the easy chair.

"How old is she, Aaron?" Lois asked.

"About eighty," he said. "I don't figure she'll last much longer."

When Nance awoke she pulled her paper bag and her Bible close to her and stared at Aaron and Lois as if they were robbers, or wild animals intent on eating her up.

Aaron took the day off and while Aaron, Jr., was in school he and Lois drove Nance the thirty-some miles from Waynesville through Jackson County to Conley's Creek. They found the cabin without much trouble. It was overgrown with kudzu vine and had a door with an old leather drawstring that was rotted and broken. Aaron got the door open and inside was a crooked, home-made table with a coal-oil lamp on it and two rickety chairs underneath. A fireplace and an ancient cast-iron stove were in the kitchen. The walls were daubed with putty and there were cracks in them big enough for birds to fly through. Dust and mold were half an inch thick on the table, where Nance set her paper bag.

"I reckon I'll need a broom," she said.

"I'll get you one," Aaron said. "We'll get some staples to get you started."

"I ain't got much money," she said.

"Let's see if you got any water," Aaron said.

They went out to the backyard and found a rusted-out washtub under a faucet. Aaron turned the tap and after a minute the water gurgled and trickled out, weak but steady. It would outlast Nance, he thought. She couldn't live more than a year or two.

There was a rotted can house, its roof falling in, and an equally decrepit outhouse. Everything was grown up in weeds and vines. Aaron opened the outhouse door and it fell off its hinges. Some wood was piled up beside the can house and there was a rusty ax leaning against the woodpile. It was a wonder nobody had taken it.

Nance just looked, taking it all in and giving out nothing.

They went back in the cabin and into the bedroom. There was a bedstead with no mattress or covers.

"I'll bring you a mattress and some quilts," Aaron said.

"Lizzy's got some, I reckon," Nance said.

"It's thirty miles to Lizzy's," Aaron said.

"I can make out," she said.

Aaron and Lois drove into Bryson City and bought

Nance some necessities, along with an extra item or two, and came back to the cabin. Nance was sitting in one of the kitchen chairs. Just sitting. Aaron was a little disappointed by her lack of enthusiasm. But then he remembered how Nance was.

Aaron drove over to Conley's Creek once a month or so and paid the rent and took Nance things she needed. She never asked for anything and seemed to get along all right with very little. She raised some game chickens that slept in the trees and pecked out a subsistence in the yard around the cabin, and she chopped her own wood and ate her own cooking. If she needed anything before Aaron came she walked the five or six miles into Bryson City, or sometimes the mail carrier—Mildred Cogburn, a red-headed, rawboned woman and a good soul—gave her a ride.

Like many other folks around Bryson City Mildred had a favorite story about Nance. It was the winter of 1939, the day before Christmas, and she was coming back from Conley's Creek into Bryson City in her mail car. It was late afternoon and it had snowed most of the day—a white Christmas, which everybody was happy about except those who had to travel. Just as Mildred came around the curve into town she saw Nance hopping along as fast as she could go. Behind her there were three kids, half-grown boys, throwing rocks and snowballs at her and hollering and calling her names.

Mildred stopped and let her in. Nance's clothes were

threadbare, with torn places in them, and she wore no coat at all. She had something in a brown paper bag clutched close under her arm.

"Why didn't you wait for me?" Mildred asked her.

"I need to go to Waynesville," Nance said.

"Waynesville? God, Nance, that's thirty miles by way of Sylva. It's shorter over Soco Gap, but it's closed because of the snow, I'm sure."

"I need to get to Waynesville," Nance repeated. Her eyes were frightened, as always.

Mildred understood that Nance was going to Waynesville if it killed her. She would never have done it for anyone else, but it was Christmas, and she had finished her deliveries, and she had always felt sorry for Nance.

"Okay," she said. "I'll take you."

"I need to go to Jonathan's Creek," Nance said.

"Okay."

A snowball with a rock in it hit the window and Nance jumped. She looked like a scared rabbit. She was about ninety years old, Mildred knew.

On the long drive to Waynesville Nance took a small, square box out of her paper bag and opened it and examined its contents. Mildred saw it was stick candy, assorted flavors. There were two broken pieces on top and with her brown little fingers Nance put them underneath the rest so they wouldn't show and the pieces on top would be perfect. She looked at Mildred suspiciously, as if she thought the younger woman would take the box away from her.

When they got to Jonathan's Creek Nance pointed the way to the Putnam cabin and Mildred pulled up into the snow-covered yard and stopped. Nance got out and hopped up the steps and laid the candy on the porch beside the door and hurried back down to the car and got in.

"Let's go," she said.

"You're not even going to see them? Or talk to them?"

"No," Nance said. "Let's go."

When Mildred got Nance back to her little shack on Conley's Creek it was night and it was still snowing, so she pulled the mail car up in such a way that the head-lights lit the path to the door. Nance held out a withered hand and opened it and inside was a quarter.

"God, Nance, it's Christmas," Mildred said.

Nance put the quarter back into her apron pocket and got out of the car and scampered up through the snow and into her shack.

> ## Dead at 104
>
> Mrs. Nancy Ann Kerley, 104, passed away Wednesday in Bryson City. She is survived by a daughter, Elizabeth Putnam of Waynesville. Burial will be in Conley's Creek Cemetery in Bryson City at 2:00 P.M. Friday.
>
> *Waynesville Clarion*, September 20, 1952

Chapter Nineteen

The mountain people left Nance alone, but stories about her continued to circulate around western North Carolina.

She had four black dogs at one time, and people said they were vicious and dangerous. Now and then someone would knock on her door and be surprised by the snarling, hungry animals.

Once a Boy Scout was separated from his troop and got lost in the woods east of Bryson City. When he was found walking down the dirt road from Conley's Creek toward town all he could talk about was the old woman he had seen hoeing corn beside the little shack, her eyes sunk back in her head. When she'd seen him she'd stopped and peered at him and scared him witless.

And there was an artist who came to Bryson City to paint the mountains. His name was Coyne and he was a retired clothing jobber from Toledo, Ohio, whose territory once included Bryson City. He had fallen in love with the mountains and the mountain people and had vowed to return and paint them. He got himself a room at the Horton Hotel and every day he went out and set up his easel and tried to capture the dark majesty of the Great Smoky Mountains in oil.

One autumn day as he was painting he saw an odd, small figure coming down the road very slowly. It was an old woman and beside her was a black dog. She carried a crooked, homemade walking stick and a black Bible. Her eyes were cavernous and her skull showed its outline through her leathery skin. As she drew near, Coyne could hardly believe that a creature so old could walk at all.

He watched with fascination as she passed and then he returned to his canvas. But it gradually dawned on him that the very qualities he was striving for, the essence of the mountains, their age, their permanence, their endurance—those qualities were embodied in the old woman.

So the next day he waited for her, but she did not appear. He waited for three days and then about noon on the fourth day his patience paid off. There she came, a small figure in black on the white dirt road.

Coyne walked up to the edge of the road and when she came close enough he spoke to her. "Ma'am?"

She stopped and peered at him. Her dog snarled and showed its yellow teeth. It looked hungry for human flesh.

"I'm a painter," Coyne said. "I'd like to paint your portrait."

"Don't need no painting done," she said.

"I'll pay you."

She just looked at him, not comprehending.

"I'll pay you five dollars to let me paint your portrait. Your picture. How about that?"

"That'd be okay, I reckon," she said, and turned away.

"Excuse me, ma'am. Where do you live?"

She stopped and turned stiffly and tried to focus on him again. "Up the road a ways," she said, and walked on.

Coyne gathered up his paints and easel and hurried back to the hotel. At dinner that night at Bryson's Grill he smiled at everyone and could hardly keep still to eat his hot roast beef sandwich, which was his favorite meal in town.

"What's got you in such a good mood?" the waitress, Dorothy, asked, freshening his coffee. Coyne liked Dorothy; she wasn't pretty but she was friendly and forthright and had a sense of humor.

"I've found something I've been looking for. Something pure and simple and good, something beautiful."

"What is it?"

"Can't tell you," Coyne said. "I'll surprise you."

"Something about your painting? I should have known. You know, you should have some fun sometime."

"Painting *is* fun, to me."

"My daddy liked to paint. Our house was every color you could think of. He'd no more than get it painted one color than he'd start in painting it some other color."

Coyne chuckled. "I don't paint houses, you know that. With my painting I'm trying to capture something. I'm trying to capture the truth."

"Sounds very grand," Dorothy said. "So what was it you saw, a raccoon? I think they're beautiful."

"I'll let you see it when I'm done," Coyne said.

The next day he drove his station wagon up the dirt road that wound up Conley's Creek until he got to the little shack. He knew the place because the black dog lay on the plank steps in front of the door. It watched him and snarled as he approached but it didn't get up. He knocked on the door and when there was no answer he opened it and went in. He found the old woman sitting alone at the table. When she saw him her eyes got big and fearful but he reminded her of who he was and coaxed her out into the front yard and set her in a chair so that behind her were the distant, majestic slopes of the Great Smokies.

After a week he had it finished. He paid the old woman and took the portrait back to his hotel room and set it up next to the window.

Tears came to his eyes as he looked at it, for in his

heart he knew he had finally done something well. He had caught the fleeting ghosts of truth and beauty, he had probed to the deep heart of life and time.

In her lap was the Holy Bible, black and solid. Beside her head was the side of the little shack, rough-hewn and tough. Beyond her were the soaring ranges of the Great Smokies. And deep within her cadaverous eyes was a tenacious—almost frightening—ember of life, still burning.

That evening he had a couple of drinks at a bar near the hotel and then dropped in at Bryson's Grill at closing time and invited Dorothy up to see the painting. When he led her into his darkened room she started to speak but he shushed her, and then he kissed her.

"Whoa," she said. "Let's remember what we're here for. I want to see this beautiful whatever-it-is."

He led her to the painting and then turned on the light and watched her face.

"Oh!" she said, and laughed, and put her hand over her mouth.

"What is it?" he asked, stunned.

"It's Nance! I mean, the painting is beautiful and all, but . . ."

"But what?"

"She's a murderer. She murdered a little child and went to prison for it."

"A murderer?"

"She buried it alive up on the side of a mountain over near Waynesville."

"My God," Coyne said. He took off his jacket and covered the painting.

"It really *is* a beautiful painting," Dorothy said, squeezing his hand.

"My God," he said.

On a chilly day in September 1952 Aaron and Lois drove up to Conley's Creek to check on Nance. Aaron pulled their '49 Ford through the tall weeds and left Lois in the car while he walked up to the front door and knocked. He waited a minute and then rapped again, harder, for he knew Nance was nearly deaf.

"Nance?" he hollered, but there was no answer, so he opened the door. The dogs were gone. She had outlived them all.

He could see that the back door was open so he walked through the house, figuring she wouldn't care. There had been a fire in the fireplace, he could tell, but it was out.

He stuck his head out the back door and looked around. Dusk was falling and the shadows were gathering. The woods behind the cabin were dark and thick and beautiful, just beginning to change to their autumn colors.

Then he saw her, a little bag of cloth and withered bones. A breeze had blown the first of the fallen leaves up around her. Beside her was a rick of wood with ten or so pine logs on it, split and quartered.

Aaron knew she was dead. He went closer and looked

at her aged face, her sunken eyes, her toothless mouth. A fly was crawling on her nose and he waved it away.

She was lying across her ax. The bony fingers of her right hand still gripped its handle.

Aaron went back through the house and out to the car. Lois was sitting with her arms folded. She rolled down her window.

"What is it?" she asked.

"Nance is dead. Out behind the house."

"Just lying there?"

"Yes."

"How terrible." She opened the door and got out. "I want to see her," she said.

"Ain't much to see."

"I want to see anyway."

He couldn't stop her so he walked with her around the side of the house. Some chickens ran up from the woods hoping to be fed. One went up and pecked at a bug on Nance's neck.

"Shoo! Get away!" Lois said. She looked at Aaron as if she expected him to say something.

"She was chopping wood when she died," he said. "She was rough as a cob, tough as saddle leather. She done wrong, but she paid for it. She survived, she lasted."

"I guess that's worth something," Lois said. "Do you think she was sorry for what she did?"

Aaron reached down and took Nance's shoulder. She was stiff. He lifted her up a little and looked under her and in her big apron pocket was her Bible.

He looked up into the woods and there was a momentary something, a movement of shadows and a muffled, shuffling sound that made the hair on the back of his neck stand up.

But it was nothing. Just the rustling of the dead leaves under his feet.

Author's Postscript

I have been very faithful to the actual facts of Roberta Putnam's murder and its aftermath, as documented in the pages of the old *Waynesville Courier*, which I unearthed in the offices of the present-day *Waynesville Mountaineer*. Another useful source was James Turpin's 1923 book, *The Serpent Slips into a Modern Eden*. A copy of that quaint, old-timey account may be found in the North Carolina Collection at the University of North Carolina at Chapel Hill.

In the court records of Haywood and Swain counties I found the bare facts of Nance's indictment, plea and sentence, as well as her death certificate, which told her date of birth, date of death, family name and so forth.

In the North Carolina Archives of the North Carolina Department of Cultural Resources, located in Raleigh, I found Nance's scant prison records. Sam Garrison, former warden and now historian of Central Prison, described the conditions Nance must have endured during her incarceration.

The story of Nance's early years is derived from local oral history, preserved in the minds of a number of mountain people who either remember the case first-hand or heard about it from their elders. I first heard it from my mother, who heard it from her mother, who saw Nance and Roberta going down through Lake Junaluska that day in February 1913. So there is necessarily an admixture of legend here, as there would be in a modern treatment of, say, the life of Jesse James, Blackbeard the Pirate or Lizzy Borden.

The story of Colonel George Kirk and his six hundred Union troops was inspired by William Medford's *Early History of Haywood County*.

The facts:

Nancy Ann Conard was born in 1848, married Howard Kerley after the Civil War and had a son by him, then left them both for Dude Hannah. By Dude she had a daughter, Elizabeth. Lizzy. Then she and Lizzy left Dude and moved in with Joe and Jane Putnam and their son, Will, who lived on the farm of a Mr. George Garrett on Jonathan's Creek. Lizzy soon had two children by Will Putnam, a boy and a girl. When the little girl, Roberta Ann, was two or so Nance took both children over Cataloochee to Hartford, Tennessee. The *Courier* relates that she brought them back to Jonathan's Creek after a few months and soon thereafter took Roberta up the side of Utah Mountain, a few miles from Maggie Valley, between Jonathan's Creek and Waynesville, ostensibly—with Will and Lizzy's approval—to put her in the county home or give her away to someone. And in fact she did try to give Roberta to the Reverend W. T. Fincher.

When Nance returned alone suspicions were generated, and after a few weeks Deputy Jack Carver arrested her along with Will and Lizzy. Lizzy was pregnant again and had her baby in jail, according to Haywood County residents who remember the case. After a search of several days Roberta was found by a boy, Frank Janes, and his dog; and Nance was then charged with first-degree murder.

No unbiased jurors could be seated from the seventy-five men who were called, for every one of them was already persuaded of Nance's guilt. And when Judge Garland S. Ferguson decided to move the trial to Bryson City, in Swain County, an angry mob formed with the intent to lynch poor Nance.

They did not prevail. After almost a year in the Swain County Jail she pled guilty to second-degree murder on the advice of her court-appointed attorney, S. A. Black of Bryson City, and was sentenced to 30 years at hard labor. She entered the Women's Division of Central Prison in Raleigh on March 6, 1914, and served 15 years, working on a dike on the Roanoke River. And carrying a Bible. She was paroled May 21, 1929, at age 80. She lived out her days on Conley's Creek, near Bryson City, and died in 1952 at age 104, when I was 7 years old.

All the photographs are authentic. The one of Nance

with the black dog was taken by Naomi Franklin of Jonathan's Creek, who was kind enough to trust me with it until I could get it copied.

So there is a preponderance of factual truth in *The Legend of Nance Dude*, but I have used some fictional devices in an effort to make the story clear and simple.

The fictions:

Elmer is fictitious, as are Jase Ledford and his family. Birch and the Phillips family are made up, too—but it was well-known at the time of the murder that Will Putnam did not accept Roberta as his own, so Birch represents a focus for Will's suspicions. Aaron Hatley and Lois Ransom and their families are invented, and so is the painter, Coyne.

"The Murdered Baby" is verbatim from the April 11, 1913, *Courier*, but most of the news articles that introduce the chapters are paraphrased for purposes of clarity and continuity. Those concerning fictional people are, of course, my invention—the item about Elmer and the bear, for example. For these reasons I have attributed all the news stories to the fictitious *Clarion*. Still, the items about Nance's crime relate the same facts as the original *Courier* articles.

Will and Lizzy rest side by side in a cemetery on Jonathan's Creek. According to their tombstones Will died in 1955 and Lizzy in 1969. Roberta lies in a different graveyard, miles away, among strangers—if, indeed, there are strangers among the dead.

Nance is buried on a grassy knoll overlooking Conley's Creek, with only a jagged black rock as her monument; but of course area residents know the grave is hers. It is a beautiful, peaceful place.

Composition by The Composing Room of Michigan

Printed and Bound by R. R. Donnelley & Sons

Designed by Debra L. Hampton

■   ■   ■